# SPRINKLES BEFORE SWEETHEARTS

# SPRINKLES
# BEFORE
# SWEETHEARTS

Coco Simon

Simon Spotlight

New York  London  Toronto  Sydney  New Delhi

This book is a work of fiction. Any references to historical events, real people, or real places are used fictitiously. Other names, characters, places, and events are products of the author's imagination, and any resemblance to actual events or places or persons, living or dead, is entirely coincidental.

SIMON SPOTLIGHT
An imprint of Simon & Schuster Children's Publishing Division
1230 Avenue of the Americas, New York, New York 10020
This Simon Spotlight edition December 2018
Copyright © 2018 by Simon & Schuster, Inc.
All rights reserved, including the right of reproduction in whole or in part in any form.
SIMON SPOTLIGHT and colophon are registered trademarks of Simon & Schuster, Inc.
For information about special discounts for bulk purchases, please contact Simon & Schuster Special Sales at 1-866-506-1949 or business@simonandschuster.com.
Text by Elizabeth Doyle Carey
Series designed by Hannah Frece
Jacket designed by Alisa Coburn and Hannah Frece
Jacket illustrations by Alisa Coburn
The text of this book was set in Bembo Std.
Manufactured in the United States of America 1118 FFG
10 9 8 7 6 5 4 3 2 1
ISBN 978-1-5344-3648-0 (hc)
ISBN 978-1-5344-3647-3 (pbk)
ISBN 978-1-5344-3649-7 (eBook)
Library of Congress Catalog Card Number 2018948321

## CHAPTER ONE
# DEAR ABBY

"Lunch is gross today," I said, lifting a piece of limp iceberg lettuce and letting it drop to my plate. I sighed and rubbed my eyes.

"Why so cranky?" asked my bestie Sierra as she chomped on some dry-looking carrot sticks.

I sighed. "I stayed up too late last night watching the World Series. My team wasn't in it, but I love postseason baseball, so my mom let me stay up. . . . Oh, oh, OH . . ." I yawned hugely, remembering to cover my mouth at the last second. "But then I couldn't wake up this morning."

"That's why you were late to class this morning?" asked MacKenzie, my newer bestie. "Because of *baseball*?" Her bright red hair was pulled up in a high ponytail, and it swung from side to side as she shook her head and faked her disapproval of me.

"Oh, shush!" I laughed and swatted at MacKenzie, who shrieked and ducked away from me. "The worst part is that I was rushing, so I forgot all this stuff I needed: my cross-country shorts, my idea notebook, my copy of *To Kill a Mockingbird*. What a hassle!"

"You *must* have been in a rush if you forgot your idea notebook!" agreed Sierra. She tossed her curly brown hair over her shoulder and smiled at someone behind me. "Hey, girls!" she said.

I turned around to see Margie and Emilia, two girls from our grade, bearing down on our table. I liked them fine—we were in art and science together—but they weren't my BFFs or anything.

"Mind if we join you?" asked Margie.

"Go for it," I said, sweeping my arm toward the empty seats at the table.

"Thanks," said Margie, setting down her tray with a smile of satisfaction.

"What's new?" asked Sierra.

"Oh, just brainstorming about the midterm project we need to make for science," said Margie, looking

2

at Emilia. Emilia nodded, but it seemed like there was something they weren't saying.

Sierra put her head into her hands. "Projects are the worst! I'm all thumbs. I hate making them."

I cleared my throat. "I love making them!" I said. It was true. I was all about crafts and DIY and would waaaay rather create a project than write a paper about something.

"What is your class's assignment?" asked Sierra. We were in different physics sections, with different teachers.

"We have to make something that shows a concept or principle in physics. Mr. Franklin said our projects can't just look good—they have to be meaningful and actually work. We have to submit our topic next week."

Margie looked at me. "What are you going to do for yours?"

I shrugged. My fingers itched to start sketching in my idea notebook, but I didn't have it today, of course. "I dunno. I'm not sure yet." I wouldn't have given out my ideas anyway, but I hadn't actually had any inspiration yet.

Margie nodded like she was perfectly satisfied

with my non-answer, and then she leaned in close. "Well, we actually sat with you today, Tamiko, because we wanted your advice about something. Right, Emilia?"

Emilia nodded, looking down at her plate of yucky food.

"If it's something about art class, I cannot help you there. Mr. Rivera—ugh! That man is a robot! I have no idea what he is looking for—" I began.

But Margie was shaking her head. "No. Actually, it's about Carlo. Right, Meels?"

Emilia blushed dark red.

"Do you want me to explain?" Margie asked her. Emilia nodded shyly.

At this point I was getting annoyed. These two had sat down and taken over my conversation with my two pals, and then one of them couldn't even speak for herself.

"What's going on?" I pushed.

"Well," said Margie, pausing dramatically and relishing the moment. "Emilia really likes Carlo. They danced together at the dance last weekend. And it wasn't just a fast dance. They slow danced too! Then Carlo asked for her SuperSnap, but he hasn't sent her a single message since then. So we're not really sure if he likes her or not."

"Aww, that's sweet," Sierra said. "Why do you like Carlo?"

Emilia didn't respond, so Margie elbowed her teasingly. "It's his dark hair, beautiful eyes, and dazzling smile, right? Anyway, what do you think? What should we do, Tamiko?"

I looked up, surprised. "What? *Me?* I don't have a clue. I barely know the guy. Why would he tell me if he had a crush on someone?"

Margie shook her head vehemently. "No, but what do you *think*? Like, what should Emilia do?"

I shrugged. This was so weird. *Who am I, Dear Abby?* "Um, ask him if he likes her?"

"Eeek!" Emilia squealed, blushing an even darker shade of red.

"No!" cried Margie. "You can't just ask someone straight up like that. That's way too direct. And what if he says yes just because he's embarrassed? He's kind of shy. Then that would set her off on the wrong course."

I sighed. "I think if you want an answer from someone, you need to ask them a direct question. Why all the playing around?"

Emilia put her face in her hands and shook her head.

No one would mistake this girl for someone pushy, so I wasn't sure what she was worried about.

Margie shook her head. "Never mind. We just thought you'd have some good advice, Tamiko, since you seem to be in the know."

"In the know about what?" *See, Margie? Ask a direct question if you want an answer from someone.*

"You know . . . boy stuff," Margie answered. "You're cool and you have guy friends and you're always wearing cute clothes, so I thought you'd know stuff about crushes."

*In the know? About guys?* I had some good guy friends from the cross-country team, but I didn't have a crush on any of them. And it was true that I loved dressing fashionably, but that's always been for *me*—I wasn't dressing to impress anyone.

I blew my bangs up from my forehead in exasperation. "Just because I have fashion sense and can talk to anyone doesn't mean I know anything about crushes."

"Oh well," Margie said. "I guess we'll just have to wait and see if Carlo sends her a SuperSnap. Or gives some other sign that he likes Emilia."

"Good luck," said MacKenzie.

Emilia nodded. "Thanks for listening," she added shyly.

We wrapped up lunch, and then Margie and Emilia left to go track down poor Carlo somewhere near the lockers.

MacKenzie, Sierra, and I stood and went to clear our trays.

"That was weird," I said, still puzzled.

"Beautiful eyes? Dazzling smile? *Carlo?*" Sierra said, and giggled.

"Wasn't it funny how it's Emilia who has the crush, but Margie did all the talking?" said MacKenzie.

Sierra nodded. "Emilia's obviously really shy, though. Poor girl. It takes a lot of courage to admit you like someone."

Even so, I couldn't imagine being in such a state that my friends would have to do all the talking for me. I was no love expert, but I knew that it was better to speak for yourself in any situation, thank you very much!

I was excited to get home after school and grab my idea notebook. I always had an idea notebook going—there was a whole shelf in my craft room filled to bursting with my used notebooks. I packed them with sketches of projects or crafts I was working on; pictures ripped from catalogs, magazines, or newspapers; ideas for ways to customize things I already had, like clothing or furniture; inspiration for my part-time job at my bestie Allie's mom's ice cream parlor, Molly's Ice Cream; and basically anything creative in my life. It's where I really let myself go. Being without it today had been like missing a limb.

I pounced on it in my room and slipped the clipped pen off the cover to chew on. I had to pen-chew when I thought. It drove my mom crazy because she always thought I was going to chip my tooth. Hadn't happened yet!

The science project was what had my wheels turning. It had to illustrate some simple physics concepts, like force, motion, and velocity. My mom had recently brought home a bunch of spools of colorful wire from one of the labs at the college where she works, and I'd been dying to

8

use them. Now I thought I could put them to use for this project. But how? With my idea due next week, I had time to come up with something really cool.

I put my pen to paper and let it roam freely while I thought about other stuff. I doodled hearts as I wondered why everyone was suddenly talking about crushes. I mean, come *on*, we were only in seventh grade! I doodled ice cream sandwiches as I thought about how much fun we'd had selling this new concoction at Molly's the day before. I doodled Roman gladiator shields as I thought about my history homework—and then my phone rang.

It was Allie herself, calling on a video chat.

"Hey!" I cried, accepting the call and grinning at Allie. I could see she was staying at her dad's that night. She and her brother alternated staying with their mom and dad. There were pluses to both locations. Her dad's new apartment had a rooftop pool, for one thing!

"Hey! Hang on while I add Sierra."

Then we were all three together. "Besties!" I said.

Ever since Allie's parents had gotten divorced and she'd had to move to a new school, the three of us had made an effort to stay close. We worked together at Molly's Ice Cream shop every Sunday, where we called ourselves the Sprinkle Sundays sisters or the Sprinkle Squad. We video-chatted at least once a day, and we tried to plan one fun thing together every week. Sometimes we missed one of these things, but we tried to keep that from happening. Otherwise we missed one another. Even though I still saw Sierra every day, it was different when it was the three of us.

"Hiiiiii!" Allie cried.

Allie asked me about the World Series (she was very supportive of my hobbies and interests, even though she could not care less about baseball), and after I filled her in, the talk turned to the two school dances she'd just attended—ours at MLK, where Allie used to go to school; and the one at Vista Green, which was her new school.

"So, Allie, can we talk about the elephant in the room?" Sierra asked.

"What are you talking about?" Allie answered.

"Colin, *duh!*" Sierra squealed. "He was in *all* of your SuperSnaps from the Vista Green dance! Anything up with that?"

Colin was one of Allie's new friends. He was the assistant editor of the school paper at Vista Green, and he'd asked her to write a weekly book review, with an ice cream recommendation to pair with each book. He was also a repeat customer at Molly's. Every time he showed up, Allie was *really* glad to see him. And since he kept showing up, I was thinking that maybe, just maybe, he was pretty glad to see her, too.

"I don't know," Allie admitted. "My other friends think he likes me, but I think he's just being nice."

I groaned inwardly as Sierra continued to grill Allie about Colin and whether they had danced together. After a while I began to zone out. I picked up my sketchbook and started drawing daggers into every heart I'd already drawn.

The only problem with video chats was, people could tell when you weren't paying attention!

"Miko?" Allie said, using my nickname. "Is this boring?"

*Busted!*

I rolled my eyes. "It's just that everyone likes someone else! I don't get what the whole deal is. Why is everyone suddenly crushing?"

"I'm not crushing," Allie said. "At least, I don't think I am."

"Well, it's all everyone talks about! At lunch it was Emilia and Carlo, and now it's this stuff about Colin. It's like . . . something's in the water. I just don't get it!"

"You mean you've never even looked at someone at school and thought they were cute? Or wondered what it would be like to go on a date with them?" Sierra's dark eyebrows were knitted close together, like she was puzzled by this.

"No! Who would I even feel that way about?"

Sierra's eyes roamed around, like she was search-ing the ceiling of her bedroom for an answer.

"Never mind," said Allie. "I need to go start my homework before my dad gets home. Don't worry about it, Tamiko. You don't need to like anyone now . . . or even ever! You'll always have friends who love you."

"So when I'm old and alone, you'll still be my friends?" I joked.

"Especially then!" said Allie. "I'll come see you with my walker!"

We all started to giggle.

"Even when I have no teeth!" Sierra howled.

"Gross!" I said, but I was laughing.

"Well, I'll still be able to eat ice cream!"

"Gotta go! Byeeeee!" said Allie, and the call ended.

I smiled. Sprinkle Sundays sisters forever!

## CHAPTER TWO
# LOOKING VERSUS SEEING

The next day in science class I watched Emilia and Carlo eyeing each other. First she'd sneak a peek at him. Then he'd dart a shy look over at her. And then they caught each other looking and they both blushed and looked down at their desks.

*Hello?* It didn't take a genius to see that they liked each other. I'd done it in just two seconds.

But the whole thing made me grouchy for some reason. As did the fact that I still hadn't come up with an idea for my science project.

Later, in art class, I felt grouchier still. Mr. Rivera was not the dragon-hearted art warrior I'd wanted for a teacher. He was a really uptight and un-fun dude who wore a dress shirt with a TIE to our class.

He was the teacher who would come to "fix" your work and paint over something you'd already done.

Just when I thought Mr. Rivera could not be more annoying . . . he got more annoying.

"Today, class, we will be working on life drawing . . . ," he droned.

*Ho hum*, I thought.

"You will be paired with a partner, and you must sketch each other's portraits. . . ."

*Yawn* . . .

"Let's see. Emilia, you're with Sarah. Jack and Brendan are together. Tamiko and Ewan . . ."

*Wait, what?*

I sat up straight in my seat, hoping that I had misheard. I looked all around as people began switching seats and scraping chairs to get close to their partners. So now not only did I have to work on a boring assignment (I don't enjoy sketching people's faces), but the face I had to sketch is Ewan, to boot! He'd been part of a group of guys who'd gotten into a sprinkles fight at the ice cream shop about a month ago, and they'd kind of trashed the place.

I mean, okay. Ewan had actually stayed to help us clean up, and he might have left some money on the counter to pay for the sprinkles, but still. Ugh. He was in the cool group at school, but being popular wasn't an excuse for being a jerk.

I was not about to budge to go sit by Ewan, so I just waited in my seat, staring at my sketch pad. Finally Mr. Rivera spotted Ewan sitting alone at his seat and asked him who his partner was.

Ewan must've mumbled my name, because Mr. Rivera kind of hitched Ewan to his feet, half dragged him across the room to me, and deposited him on a stool that had recently been vacated by Sarah.

I looked at Ewan and let out a big sigh of aggravation to let him know that I was not happy with this pairing. He looked away.

We sat there until Mr. Rivera called, "Tamiko and Ewan, let's see pencils moving on paper, please!"

I jerked my sketch pad off the table, huffed as I grabbed my pencil, and scowled as I turned to face Ewan. I wanted him to know that I hadn't forgotten about the sprinkles incident and that I did not like him in any way, shape, or form.

Ewan lifted his pad and began moving his pencil along the paper. I set my jaw and did the same, trying to look at him as little as possible.

We did not speak.

A minute passed.

Okay, it was really hard to draw someone without looking at him.

Because I was good at art and creative stuff, I couldn't just sit there and do a bad job. I decided I'd simply do the sketch looking at Ewan as little as possible—it would be like a test for my visual memory. I stole a glance at Ewan, hardly lifting my eyes. Then I quickly looked back at my paper and tried to capture the shape of his head.

I could not feel him looking at me, so he must've also been in stealth mode.

His hair on top was black and spiky, so that made his head shape kind of confusing. I really had to look to get it right. Again, I peeked and looked away quickly; his ear was stumping me too, hidden as it was by a chunk of his black hair. Actually, now that I looked, his hair was more a dark, dark brown than black. More like . . . dark chocolate.

I hated dark chocolate. It was like a trick: you thought it was going to taste sweet—because *chocolate*—but then it didn't!

As I sketched, I worked my way down from his

hair to his forehead. Ewan had no acne or anything, which was good, because would I have had to draw it, if so? That could have been awkward and gross, studying his zits to get them right. Still, I was jealous that his skin was so flawless.

His eyebrows were also dark brown. They were strong, like slash marks above his eyes. I wanted to get their angles right, so I just—

Ugh! He caught me looking! We both froze and then quickly looked back at our pads. But I needed another peek in order to keep going.

So I looked up, and then he looked up and we locked eyes.

"What?" I said defiantly.

He shook his head. "N . . . Nothing!" he shot back. He looked down at his pad again.

"I'm just trying to get this right so Mr. Rivera won't give me an F," I huffed.

He looked up again. "Yeah. Me too."

I snorted a little, like, *Yeah, I'm sure your drawing will be terrible because you're this popular guy and you probably think it's cool to be bad at art.* Then I used the opportunity to really nail down the angle of those eyebrows. I could see that they almost kind of angled up at the ends, now that I studied them.

He looked at me carefully, like he was going to say something, his eyes roving back and forth across my face.

"What?" I asked.

He shrugged and went back to drawing, which made me even madder. You can't just ignore people's questions!

And then I remembered that Ewan had never even apologized for the sprinkles fight. Now would have been the perfect time for him to say he was sorry. Like my mom always said—better late than never. But Ewan just sat there, drawing away on his sketch pad. I couldn't believe how rude this guy was.

Mr. Rivera called out, "Tamiko! Keep that pencil moving, please!"

Leave it to Mr. Rivera to make my sour mood even worse.

I put my pencil to the paper once again and looked at Ewan's downcast eyes. They were set widely apart and deep in his face, with a sharp up-and-down line on the inside, and they narrowed as they got out to the ends, far from his nose. His lashes were very long and dark. Like, I had never realized that boys could have such long eyelashes. I knew some high school girls who wore fake lashes that were long and curly. Ewan's were already so long that he would never need to wear fake ones. I almost giggled, imagining Ewan with ridiculously long eyelashes like a camel.

But how would I draw the lashes over his eyes? Maybe I should've paid more attention to the portrait examples that Mr. Rivera had showed us earlier. Oops. I lightly sketched in his eyes, planning to come back to them, and then I worked my way down his nose. The mouth was tricky because it's a little awkward to stare someone right in the mouth for any period of time.

As I peeked, I saw that Ewan had a very light shadow of a mustache above his upper lip. *Should I draw that in?* I wondered. Was that something that was kind of embarrassing for him, or did boys get psyched when they started to show signs of manhood? Who knew? But then I remembered: this was Ewan. Ee-wahn. Why did I suddenly care if I offended him? I sketched in his mustache, maybe even a little more than I should have. After all, it was there, wasn't it?

Gliding my pencil tip across the paper, I tried to feather in Ewan's eyelashes. I didn't feel Mr. Rivera come up behind me, so I was startled when he spoke just near my shoulder.

"Lovely work on the eyelashes, Tamiko. You've captured the beauty of Ewan's eyes perfectly."

*The beauty of Ewan's eyes?*

I wanted to scream! Ewan didn't have beautiful eyes! Mr. Rivera was totally nuts. Even if Ewan *had* had beautiful eyes, I certainly would not have noticed that or tried to "capture" it!

I thought of what Margie had said about Carlo's looks. Everything about it sounded made-up, like it was some article in a celebrity magazine—beautiful eyes, dazzling smile.

We were talking about seventh-grade boys here, people!

I was done with my drawing.

I slapped the pad onto the table and turned away from Ewan.

"Wait!" he said. "Don't move! I'm almost done!"

"Too bad!" I said. "Time's up." I was surprised that he'd asked me to keep posing, though. I never would have done that if the shoe had been on the other foot. Like, "Hey, hold still while I keep staring at you."

Luckily, just then Mr. Rivera stood at the front of the room and called out, "Okay, students! That's it for today!"

There were groans across the class, but I think they were more like groans of displeasure at the work people had produced than groans of unhappiness that class was over.

Mr. Rivera went on. "I want you to think about just *looking* versus really *seeing*. When you study someone, you see them in a different way and you can learn more about them than you can from just superficial looking. There's always more than meets the eye at first glance."

Ewan's eyelashes sprang to mind, but I quickly pushed that thought out of my head.

"What you think you see and what's really in front of you are sometimes different things," continued Mr. Rivera.

*Not really!* I saw a bratty, popular guy who thought he was hot stuff, who had come into Molly's Ice Cream and thrown sprinkles all over and made a huge mess. And that was who Ewan was, sprinkles-cleaner or no sprinkles-cleaner. Fancy eyelashes or no fancy eyelashes.

"For homework this week, sketch what you think you remember about your partner's face. Next week we'll take the portraits to the next stage—finished line art," said Mr. Rivera.

*Wait, we'll be doing this next week too?*

My hand shot into the air. "How long are we doing this project for?" I called out.

"Please don't call out, Tamiko. This portrait unit will carry over the next three classes," said Mr. Rivera. "Your final product will be displayed in the middle school art show in one month's time, so give it your all!"

Three more classes staring at Ewan.

I wanted to be sick right then and there. I gathered up my things and hustled out of the room without even a backward glance.

## CHAPTER THREE
# LOVEBIRDS

The week passed slowly as I tried to come up with a cool idea for my science project and also tried to avoid looking at the Ewan drawing in my art sketch pad. Why did I have to spend my precious time drawing sketches of Ewan?

Allie's and Sierra's reactions when I told them I was partnered with Ewan were just as I had suspected they'd be: horrified!

"Oh, Miko, I can't believe you have to even talk to him, never mind be his partner!" sympathized Allie over video chat.

"At least he's easy on the eyes!" joked Sierra.

"I am not even responding to the stupidity of that comment!" I said, indignant.

On Thursday after school I had a snack and then slunk up to my crafts closet to let loose for a little while. I was shortening an old kilt I'd found at a thrift shop, and then I was going to appliqué a puffy pale-pink rose onto it. When I was done, the skirt would look very punk rock and cool with footless black tights.

I was also painting a cheap pair of white Keds that I'd gotten on sale. I was lightly drawing graffiti art all over them, and then I was going to airbrush in some color once I was happy with the design. My other big thing right then was custom picture frames . . . made with candy. I'd pick a colorful kind of candy—like gummi bears or candy corn—and then I'd glue the pieces to a white picture frame and shellac the whole thing. (I had to do that part outdoors, I learned the hard way, because *fumes*.)

I sat down in the spinning chair that I'd thrifted from the upcycling area of the dump. It was ergonomic and super-comfy. Actually, I was going to customize it, too. It was just plain black, like an office chair. It could use some feathers and strings of beads hanging off it, I thought. My taste was to customize things in the opposite style of what they were. So a businesslike office chair would get the bohemian treatment, and a scary-looking leather jacket would get a painting of a fluffy teddy bear on the back. Get it?

Turning from side to side, I thought about physics. Things moving, speeding, spinning, gravity acting on mass, all that stuff. I stopped turning and unspooled some of the beautiful cobalt-blue wire my mom had brought home. The other wires were just as brilliant: a rich red with tiny white stripes on it, bright orange with jade-green horizontal stripes across it, a solid plummy purple, and a bold pink. My fingers itched to do something cool with them all.

I sat and played with the length of blue wire, hoping it would inspire me. Seeing all the different colors in the spools made me think of the string that Allie, Sierra, and I had used to make friendship bracelets back in elementary school. I had made a turquoise-and-white bracelet for Allie, and a blue-and-pink one for Sierra. Hmmm. Friendship bracelets were cool, but they didn't demonstrate any physics.

I crumpled the wire into a ball and pitched it in the general direction of my trash can. Then I ran downstairs to say hi to my parents, who had just arrived home from work.

"Mommy! Daddy!" I called. Half the time I liked to call my parents "Mommy" and "Daddy" as a joke. This helped butter them up for the rest of the time, when I called them by their first names, Ayumi and Toshi. I thought that using their names made me sound more grown-up, but my parents hated it.

"Hello, Tamiko," said my mom, setting a bag of groceries on the counter.

I peeked inside. "What's for dinner?"

"Salad and fondue," said my dad.

"Yum! I love fondue night!"

"Good. Then you can start cutting up the bread while I cut the veggies," said my mom, thrusting two baguettes at me.

"I mean, I hate fondue night! Yuck!"

My dad chuckled and grabbed a seltzer from the fridge, then sat down at the table. "Ah. Busy day," he said, relaxing.

My mom went to stand behind him and rub his shoulders. He sighed in appreciation.

"Gross! Too much PDA!" I said. My parents were always goofy and silly with each other, and it could be so embarrassing.

"Oh, does this bother you?" teased my mom,

leaning down and planting a smooch on my dad's cheek.

"Disgusting!" I gagged.

My parents laughed. "Tamiko, seriously. You should be happy your dad and I love each other."

"Keep it to yourselves," I said as I rolled my eyes. But she was right. I couldn't imagine what it would be like if my parents were divorced, like Allie's.

My dad started singing this love song out loud in a really bad voice, all out of tune and sappy, and my mom was giggling away as I made gagging sounds over the cutting board.

The back door slammed, and my older brother, Kai, walked in.

"Thank goodness you're here!" I called. "Save me!"

Kai looked at my parents and laughed as he dropped his jacket and backpack onto the bench and took off his shoes by the door. "The lovebirds getting to you?" he said.

That prompted my dad to start in on some hideous new song about lovebirds. I put my hands over my ears. "Make them stop!"

My parents were laughing their heads off now.

"Why does everybody have to be in love all the time?" I wailed, and stamped my foot.

"I'm not in love," said Kai, grabbing a chunk of baguette and popping it into his mouth. "That's because there's only one person I love—me!"

"Oh boy. Nice to be modest!"

He shrugged. "What can I say? Either you've got it or you don't."

Dinner was delicious, except my dad insisted on creating a rule that if you accidentally dropped your bread into the fondue pot, you had to kiss the person sitting on your left.

This time Kai was on my side. "No way!" he said, shaking his head.

"Come on. It's a real fondue tradition from Switzerland!" my dad said, but he might have just been making that up.

"What's the problem? We're all family here. Right, Tamiko?" my mom said, and leaned her cheek toward me like she was waiting for a kiss.

I pushed her away. "You're not even sitting on my left!"

Kai and I were extra careful and didn't drop a

single piece of bread during the meal. I briefly wondered if the rule had been a ploy to give us better table manners, but my dad dropped his bread and had to kiss my mom three times—so I think it was just them being silly lovebirds again.

After dinner Grandpa Sato called us at the usual time. He was my grandpa who lived in Japan. Since we barely ever got to visit him, we made a point to video-chat him every night.

He and I spent some time dissecting all the important moments from the previous night's World Series game. Grandpa Sato was also a huge baseball fan. He even subscribed to a certain sports channel so he could watch American baseball on his TV.

"Are you going to go see a game soon?" I asked. About once or twice a season, my grandpa and his friends went to a Japanese professional baseball game. I secretly wished I had friends who would go watch a game with me. Sierra and Allie would probably go if I invited them, but I didn't want to drag them to something they thought was boring.

"Perhaps," replied Grandpa Sato. "I'm not as young as I used to be. The train ride to the baseball stadium is very long, and there are many steps to get to the bleachers."

I bit my lip. Grandpa Sato had arthritis, and I could tell his knees were bothering him more than they used to. Most of the time I tried not to think about how old he was getting.

Then Grandpa Sato's eyes twinkled. "Don't worry about me! I'll stay nice and healthy, so that I can attend your wedding one day. My sweet Tamiko as a beautiful bride!"

He said this to me all the time, but that day it really bugged me. "What if I don't want to be a bride?" I said fiercely. "There's already too much romance around me. I can barely handle it."

Grandpa Sato laughed. "There can never be such a thing as too much love in the world."

I pouted. "Well, I don't want to get married."

"That's fine!" Grandpa said. "Because you'll never love anyone more than me, right?" He chuckled. I sighed. Everyone thought love was soooo funny.

My parents made me finish all my homework before I could go down and watch the next World Series game that night.

I was debating about telling them how I was stumped with my science project, but then I worried that they'd just get all bossy with me and try to take over. They loved school projects.

I kept my mouth shut, but my brain was whirring as I sat and watched. Maybe there'd be something in the game that would inspire me. Maybe I could do a project about baseballs and bats and the trajectory of the ball when it was hit a certain way.

But instead of being excited and inspired by the game, the opposite happened. Sometime during the seventh inning just before a commercial break, the camera zoomed in on a young man down on one knee in the stands. He pulled out a ring and held it out to the woman sitting next to him. It was a marriage proposal!

She said yes, and the whole place went crazy as the footage of them hugging flashed on the JumboTron with the word YES!!! blinking over it in bright red.

"Ugh. Here we go again! More love!" I said. "Way to ruin a baseball game, dude!"

Kai looked at me incredulously. "Jeez, they just got engaged. Let them celebrate!"

"Love has no place in baseball." I was indignant.

"Love is everywhere!" said my dad, the romantic. "The fans love the players—or most of them anyway. The players love one another—or some of them do. Everyone loves the sport."

"Okay, romantic love has no place in baseball, then!" I cried.

"Jeez!" said my dad this time. "What a grump you are."

"What's wrong with you?" asked Kai.

"Nothing. It's all of you who have something wrong!" I crossed my arms over my chest and huffed until my mom came in with a big bowl of buttered popcorn, and then I, too, felt love. For the popcorn, that is.

But later that night Kai's words echoed in my head. *Was* there something wrong with me? Why couldn't I stand all this love stuff? Did everyone else on earth like it but me?

My parents loved being in love. The couple at the baseball game had looked ecstatic. Grandpa Sato wanted me to marry. Emilia swooned over Carlo. Even Allie and Sierra thought it was fun to talk about love.

What was the deal?

## CHAPTER FOUR
# THE SPRINKLE SUNDAYS TASTE TEST

Sunday was my happy time. The three Sprinkle Sundays sisters were reunited and together again at Molly's.

It was such a beautiful store—with blue-and-cream-striped seats and awnings, a black-and-white tiled floor, cool ice cream cone light fixtures and design elements, and incredibly yummy ice cream flavors. The ones I'd tried so far, at least.

I clocked into work ten minutes early. Allie was already there, and Sierra joined us right after—on time, which was rare. It felt good to all be there at the right time, since we'd had a bunch of small fights about being late in the past. Sometimes I was the one who was late (usually because I was trying to finish a project at home), and sometimes it was Sierra (usually because she was overcommitted), and Allie had to be the bad guy and yell at us.

But not today! We happily got ready for our shift—cleaning up, making toppings, prepping some sundae supplies. And then we waited for the post-lunch rush.

But it never came.

After our first hour we'd had only one customer. Usually we'd get at least a dozen people in our first hour, but sometimes way more. We'd had entire soccer teams show up, creating lines out the door.

At first we stood at attention, sure that the rush was about to begin. But as the hour dragged by, we each looked for projects to keep us busy.

"I'm going to organize the supply closet," I said. Shifting around tubs of sprinkles and boxes of cones and plastic bowls was better than standing around doing nothing.

"I'm going to clean the bathroom," said Sierra with a shrug.

You know things are bad when someone volunteers to clean a bathroom.

Neither of us wanted to say anything out loud,

since the store was new and we didn't want to hurt Allie's feelings by implying that business wasn't good. But after Sierra and I finished our projects (ten minutes killed!), we regrouped behind the counter and gingerly explored the topic of the store's emptiness.

Sierra looked out the window. "Kind of a chilly day. Maybe not great ice cream weather."

Allie frowned. "We've had chilly days before, though."

"Maybe it's because it's chilly and *cloudy*," I said. "People aren't feeling like being out and about. They're hunkered down."

"Yes, but they could come get takeout," said Allie. "Pints or gallons to have at home. It's not so much about, 'Oh, hey, let's go get ice cream' as an activity. It should be more like, 'I am so obsessed with that Saint Louis Cake ice cream that I have to have it right now.' You know?"

Sierra and I both nodded, but I wasn't sure if those cravings would actually convince people to get off their couches and leave the house.

I sighed, and Sierra wiped the counter for the eighth time. Just then Mrs. Shear came in from her office in the back. "How's it going, girls?"

Allie shook her head slowly. "Not great, Mom. We've only had one customer today so far."

"One customer!" Mrs. S. put her hands on either side of her face. "That's terrible! Sunday is usually our busiest day." She crossed the floor to look out the window. "Pretty quiet out there today." She folded her arms across her chest and watched the street. "Let's see. We've done coupons, pet-adoption drives, social media promos, fancy themed sundaes and cones, publicity . . ." She tapped her foot as she thought.

"Maybe we need some new flavors to showcase?" I suggested.

"Maybe." Allie pressed her lips together. "I think the current flavors are really good, though."

"I've actually been thinking of adding new flavors to the menu," Mrs. S. said. "Something sophisticated, like crème brûlée."

"What's that?" asked Sierra.

"A fancy French dessert. It's a vanilla custard with a crackling caramelized sugar coating on top."

"I think your new flavor should be kid-friendly," Sierra offered. "Just because they're, like, the majority of our customers."

Mrs. S. nodded. "True. Do you girls have any ideas

for new flavors? My brain is frozen!" She laughed. "Get it? Frozen like ice cream?"

"Moooom!" groaned Allie, and we all laughed. Then we stood thinking in silence for a minute.

"What about Hot Chocolate Marshmallow, since it's starting to get cold out?" suggested Sierra.

"That is a cute idea, but we already sell Rocky Road. It's kind of the same thing," said Allie.

"Not really, though, because Rocky Road has nuts," I offered.

"Oh, Rocky Road has nuts?" said Sierra. "I've never tried it."

"Girls! You need to sample all of our products! How will you ever be able to sell them if you don't?" said Mrs. S. with a smile.

"Maybe we should each take a tiny spoonful of each one and then rate them," I suggested.

"Totally!" agreed Sierra.

We looked at Allie expectantly. She usually had some reason why our ideas would cost the store money. When I was having a good day, I thought of her as a smart businesswoman. When I was having a bad day, she just seemed like a killjoy. Today I held my breath, awaiting her response.

"Yes," agreed Allie. "It'll be like a taste test. Is that okay, Mom?"

"Go for it," said Mrs. S. "I'm eager to hear the results."

To create our ice cream rating system, I pulled out my idea notebook and made a table with the flavor names running down the side and each of our names running across the top. Then we agreed to taste each flavor with a mini-spoon and rate it on a scale of one to five for flavor and one to five for originality. This was the list of that day's flavors:

- Kitchen Sink (vanilla ice cream with crumbled pretzels and potato chips)
- Hokey Pokey (with bits of honeycomb toffee)
- Strawberry Shortcake
- Banana Pudding
- Lavender Blackberry
- Chocolate Mint Chip
- Peppermint
- Candy Bar
- Lime Sorbet
- Balsamic Strawberry

- Butterscotch Chocolate Chunk
- Rocky Road
- Saint Louis Cake
- Vanilla
- Chocolate
- Lemon Blueberry
- Cereal Milk
- Cinnamon (with crumbled lace butter cookies in it)

We worked our way through the case, taking our time and discussing each flavor. I was very partial to the chocolaty flavors, while Sierra really loved the fruity ones best. Allie loved them all, for different reasons.

It was funny, but the best part of the test was that it pushed all of us out of our comfort zones. Like, I would never normally have ordered Balsamic Strawberry or Lavender Blackberry, and Sierra had never tried Rocky Road or Kitchen Sink. Allie had tried them all but was in a bit of a flavor rut, so it opened her mind back up to what we had to offer. We also saw which ice creams we needed to push the customers to try, because we were definitely underselling amazing flavors we hadn't even known we liked.

"I don't know about that Rocky Road," Sierra said when it was time to try that one. "It's kind of gross-looking."

"Why? Because it's all lumpy and gooey?" said Allie. "Sometimes you have to look carefully at something, because superficial first impressions can be wrong. Like, see this white goo that looks like bird droppings? It's actually a thick streak of soft marshmallow. Your eyes are telling you one thing, but maybe your taste buds will tell you another."

Sierra shrieked at the "bird droppings" comment but tried the ice cream anyway. She chewed thoughtfully and then nodded her head. "Yes. I get it now. It's actually really delicious. Kind of salty and sweet, creamy yet crunchy. Gooey all over. It tastes *much* better than it looks. Its appearance doesn't do it justice."

We moved on down the case, flavor by flavor.

"I can't believe we're getting paid to do this!" I said dreamily.

"We're the luckiest girls in the world," agreed Sierra.

"Group hug!" called Allie. We paused for a big hug. Sometimes we were kind of dorks that way, but when you don't get to be all together with your best friends every day, you've got to take hugs when you can get them.

In the end the flavor with the highest marks overall was . . . wait for it . . . Banana Pudding! "Do you think I could have a little more?" I asked Allie. "I mean, if I could make a sundae, I'd pay for it."

Allie seemed like she was going to just say no automatically, but at the last second she reversed course. "Let me go ask my mom," she said instead.

Sierra and I looked at each other as Allie left. Sierra shrugged, and I raised my eyebrows. We were pretty surprised that Allie was up for it.

Allie returned seconds later. "She said yes. She doesn't want the product sitting around getting old. She said turnover is half the battle here and that we should each go ahead and make ourselves a sundae."

"Wow! Thanks, Ali-li!" I said, hugging Allie again. "This is so fun! I'm going to see if I can create a new featured sundae to put on social media."

I set about getting a bowl and layering in some broken cones that we crushed and kept in a bin for just that purpose. Then I scooped out two big, round scoops of the creamy, thick, and custardy Banana

Pudding. It had chunks of Nilla wafers throughout that had grown chewy and dense from the heavy cream soaking into them, and it was chock-full of nuggets of real banana. The Banana Pudding flavoring was intense and rich, and I added a sprinkling of dry, crushed Nilla wafers from our toppings bar over the top of the sundae for a texture contrast.

"Hmmm," I said. "I think I'm done. Should I add hot fudge, or is that overkill?"

"Overkill," said Sierra firmly.

The door jingled just then, and a young couple walked into the store. The three of us jumped to attention as they surveyed the case.

"What should we get? What do you girls like best here?" the young woman asked.

"Funny you should mention it," I said. "We just decided that we like Banana Pudding the best. Would you like to try our Banana Pudding sundae? I just made it." I put it on top of the counter for the couple to inspect.

"Wow. Sure, that looks delicious!" the man said with a happy grin.

Hurray! I loved it when customers took me up on my flavor recommendations. I was always trying to get people to order more interesting things, outside of their comfort zones. "Will that be two Banana Pudding sundaes, then?" I confirmed.

"Oh no, we'll just share one," the woman answered, and the couple smiled at each other.

I tried not to roll my eyes, since they were our precious customers. But here was the bazillionth piece of evidence that everyone was crazy in love.

The couple sat down at a table to eat their ice cream. I couldn't help noticing that they weren't just sharing the sundae—they were also sharing the spoon to eat it! Gross! I wasn't a germophobe or anything, but it seemed so unnecessary. Why would you want to taste someone else's spit when you're trying to enjoy the delicious Banana Pudding goodness?

I must have been staring too much, because Allie elbowed me in the side and told me to look busy. I casually strolled over to the utensil jar and refilled it with spoons. Hint, hint. Nudge, nudge.

When the couple had finished the sundae, they thanked me for the flavor recommendation again. It was nice of them, and it almost made up for their sundae- and saliva-sharing . . . almost.

"And we had the store to ourselves too!" The

couple laughed. "Last time we came, it was so busy that there was nowhere to sit."

"Please come again!" Allie called as the couple left the store. But as soon as the door closed, her smile faded. "It felt like they were rubbing it in that we didn't have any other customers."

"I don't think they meant it that way," Sierra said, soothing her.

"Allie has a point," I said. "It's like the opposite of knowing that a restaurant has good food when it has a long line. If the store always looks empty, customers might wonder if there's a reason why no one's eating here. They might not come back."

There was a heavy silence among us.

"We need to do some market research for our new flavor," I said finally. "Like, finding out what flavors are popular with young kids . . ."

"And young parents," added Allie. "I wish there were somewhere we could go where we'd be surrounded by kids and their parents eating. Then we could see what they like to order."

"What about the food truck courtyard at the Commons?" asked Sierra. The Commons was a mall near us, and we loved to go there for lunch or an early dinner on Saturdays. The food trucks featured flavors from all around the world, so it could feel like you were on vacation when you ate there. But that place was mostly for teenagers and younger adults, not parents with young kids.

"Hey! What about Felton Pier? There's always a lot of kids there," Allie said.

Felton Pier was a carnival on a boardwalk in a town about forty-five minutes down the coast from us. It had rides and fancy carnival food and cool games for good prizes. We used to go for one another's birthdays when we were little, but most of the rides were a little too kiddie for us now. I hadn't been in a few years.

"Perfect!" Sierra cried, putting both fists straight up in the air. "Every kid likes carnival food, and we can see what's selling the most there. Let's do it!"

"We could go next Saturday," I suggested. "I hope all our parents say yes! And I hope we can get one of them to drive us. It's sort of a hike."

"I bet my dad will do it," offered Allie. "He's always looking for ways to spend more time with me, especially these days."

I hooked my arm around her neck and squeezed.

I didn't need to say anything. She knew I was hugging her to say I still loved her and I loved her parents even if they weren't married, and it was all going to be okay.

At the end of our shift, Mrs. S. came out to pay us, and Allie told her our Felton Pier idea.

"Sounds like a great idea!" agreed Mrs. S. "I'll even give you all some cash to cover your research fees. How will you girls get there?"

"I'll ask Dad if he can drive," replied Allie. Mrs. S. smiled, but she also looked slightly disappointed. I wondered if Mrs. S. felt the same way as Mr. S., that she never had enough time to spend with Allie.

"I'll bring my notebook to write down all of our great ideas!" I said.

"Assuming all our parents say yes and my dad can drive us, let's all meet here around noon on Saturday. Okay?" suggested Allie.

"O-*yay*!" I cried.

## CHAPTER FIVE
# SKETCHY SECRET

I was so psyched to have a fun weekend plan that I could look forward to all week. When I got home that night and asked my parents if I could go, they said yes! I immediately texted the news to my besties. Sierra said her parents had agreed too, and Allie said her dad had offered to drive us, as expected.

I'd already finished my homework and I still had some time before dinner, so I headed to my craft room. I simply had to come up with an idea for the science project; it was driving me nuts. *Don't overthink it, Tamiko,* I could hear Allie saying.

But how could I not? Overthinking projects was what I did best!

I needed to keep my hands busy while trying to

come up with a supercool science idea in my note-book. Inspiration didn't strike if you were just staring at a blank piece of paper! I pulled out my decoupage supplies and began thinking of how I could decorate the cover of my idea notebook. Decoupage was basi-cally an extra-fancy collage: you cut pictures out of a magazine or greeting card or whatever, pasted the pictures to a surface, and then shellacked or laminated over them to protect the images.

I kept envelopes filled with different images, sorted by type. I had an envelope of flowers I'd cut out, desserts that looked delish, kittens, race cars, and pugs. For this idea notebook, I chose carnival-themed images: a roller coaster sticker, a postcard from Coney Island, and a huge ice cream appliqué, of course! Within an hour my idea notebook looked amazing and Felton Pier–ready.

But I still had no science project idea.

Dissatisfied, I left the craft room and went to check on dinner.

"Tamiko, honey, please come chop some veggies for dinner," said my dad.

"What are we having?" I asked, sniffing the air. It smelled homey and warm.

"Udon," he said.

"Yay! Great idea, Toshi!"

"Don't call me Toshi, kid."

"Okay, Tosh."

My dad rolled his eyes, and I grinned.

Udon was a type of Japanese noodle. The noodles were thick and chewy, and you could add all kinds of toppings—mushrooms, fish cakes, eggs, and more. The broth was rich and salty. It made you feel strong and loved when you ate it.

My dad handed me some bok choy, scallions, and big mushrooms. "Wash well, then chop. I don't want any grit in my udon. Get it, kid?" he said in a fake-gruff voice.

"Got it, Tosh," I joked.

"Use the salad spinner to dry the bok choy after."

I ran the water in the kitchen sink, and the rushing sound relaxed me. I let my mind wander back over the day and the incredible flavors that had passed through my mouth. Then I thought about the couple who'd wanted to share everything, even their spoon.

"Toshi?" I said.

"Mmm-hmm-don't-call-me-Toshi," my dad said automatically.

"How old were you when you had your first crush?" I rinsed the bok choy carefully, parting the leaves to let the water spray into every crevice and chase away the grit. Then I plopped it into the salad spinner and pumped.

My dad stopped what he was doing and thought. "My first real crush?"

I nodded. Then I set aside the bok choy and worked on the scallions, peeling away the outermost layer of each one and washing the goo and sand off the stems.

"Mmm, probably fourteen or fifteen. I was kind of a late bloomer," he said, and shrugged.

"Oh!" I said. *Phew,* I thought. I shook the water off the scallions and began wiping the mushrooms with a wet paper towel.

"Why?" he asked, turning to look at me. "Are you thinking of eloping?"

"Gross! I don't even know what that means!"

My dad chuckled. "Good. Because it means running away to get married without your parents' permission."

"Haha. I don't even like anyone!" I kept my head down, laying out the cutting board and chop-chop-chopping the scallions.

He turned back to the noodles he was preparing. "Oh yeah? I think that's good."

"You do?" I stopped chopping and looked up at him.

"Yeah," he said, turning to look at me too. "When you have a crush, it's really fun and exhilarating. You hope all day to see the person. You plan witty things to say to them. You wonder if they feel the same way about you. It adds some excitement to your life, especially if they like you back."

"Oh," I said. That sounded kind of nice.

"But it can also be very distracting. Sometimes it can take your attention away from important things in your life, like school and family and friends."

"Oh. That doesn't sound good." *It also makes you look silly,* I thought, picturing Emilia's bright red blush around Carlo. "Maybe I'll just avoid crushes forever."

"Well, it's not really something you can control. But it's also not something you can force or fake. Don't feel like you have to like someone just because it's the trend, you know?"

I shrugged. "I guess."

"When I was your age, all my friends liked this famous pop singer, a young woman in her twenties.

But I didn't understand what the big deal was. She was all grown up, and she sang songs about heartbreak that I could not relate to at all. I ended up pretending I was crazy about her too, to go along with all my friends. But then one day I had to draw the line."

"Wow, Tosh—Dad. Why? What made you do that?"

My dad laughed. "Her concert tickets cost a fortune, and I couldn't summon up the desire to beg my parents for the money. I told my friends that my parents didn't approve of my love for the woman, and they all understood. The concert was kind of a bust for my friends, too. The singer lip-synced the whole thing and didn't even smile once. In the end I looked wise for saving my money and not going. All the other kids regretted it."

"Ha!" I laughed. "Smart!"

"Well, I looked smart by accident, but I was lucky. The point is, I felt bad that I had to kind of lie and pretend to my friends that I liked someone, just to fit in. I should have had the courage to be honest about my feelings. I don't think my friends would have cared a whit if I wasn't as enchanted as they were by this celebrity. You shouldn't ever fake affection or love. The feelings will come when it's time."

What did that even mean, "the feelings will come when it's time"? It sounded so vague. What if that "time" never came?

My dad ruffled my hair. "Just be yourself. That's who everyone loves. Now give me those veggies, please! And hand me the salad spinner so I can drain it."

I handed him the spinner and suddenly thought, *Hmmm. Physics project? Something that spins could show centrifugal force.*

*But do I really want to have an old salad spinner as my project?*

After our delicious dinner I took the salad spinner up to my room to play around with it. I liked how it spun, but I didn't see how I could re-create it in any fresh way. Like, why not just bring in the salad spinner itself?

Stumped, I set it aside and looked through my science textbook and handouts. Nothing inspired me. It was so weird. I'd heard of writer's block, but this was like scientist's block.

Sighing, I put my books back into my school-bag and noticed my art sketch pad. Mr. Rivera had asked us to sketch our portrait subject from memory over the week, but I felt weird spending my free time working on a picture of Ewan at home.

I flipped open the sketch pad and looked at my drawing of Ewan. I felt a fluttery nervousness in my chest and snapped the pad shut. Obviously, my drawing would turn out beautifully because I was an artist. But what if Ewan saw it in art class? He'd think that I actually wanted to capture the so-called *beauty of his eyes.*

Picking up my idea notebook instead, I opened it to a blank page. I could do a couple of sketches of Ewan in there. Then, if Mr. Rivera asked to see my work in art class, I could show him that. But if he *didn't* ask, no one would be the wiser, and I'd never be caught by Ewan. My own little secret sketchbook. *A sketchy secret,* I thought, and giggled, but then my mood darkened as I began to try to draw Ewan's face from memory. All I could picture was him throwing sprinkles at Molly's.

It was tough to remember the specifics of his face at first. Certain features seemed more prominent in my mind than others (like the eyelashes, annoyingly), while other things that I'd never really gotten right—like the shape of his head—were hard to capture. Then, for some reason, I got it into my head that he had a dimple in his cheek, but I wasn't sure. I put it in and took it out, then put it back in. I'd have to check the next time I saw him, without him noticing, of course. Thinking of Ewan that much made me grouchier still.

Bored with trying to be accurate, I got creative instead. I did one drawing in a manga style, with Ewan as a bad guy in a spiky-collared black cape and those slashy dark brown eyebrows of his. Then I did a series of comic panels, with Ewan styled as the villain fighting the superhero (me, of course) and shooting sprinkles from his wrists. I also did a sketch that was all angles and straight lines, like an Ewan robot, and another that was super-rounded and bubble-shaped, like a Saturday morning cartoon character. It was actually fun to try out the different drawing styles, and I killed about forty-five minutes drawing ten pages' worth of pictures of Ewan, of all things. The results were actually pretty satisfying, and that helped lighten my dark mood in the end. I thought, *He should be thankful that his partner is such a good artist*—even though I wasn't thankful for *him*.

Art homework done, I stretched and got up to pack my bag and decide my outfit for school the next day. People at school had high expectations for what I wore—especially on a Monday, when I'd had the whole weekend to put a look together—so the bar was pretty high. Plus, this week more than ever, my outfit choice mattered. After all, my outfit might be immortalized in Ewan's drawing of me.

I pulled out my fake-leather motorcycle jacket as my anchor piece, to build the look around. The hardness of the jacket and all its metal and buckles called for something soft and feminine to balance it. I chose a granny dress in a floral print that I'd shortened way high and hitched up in uneven gathers around the hemline. It was really cool. Then I picked out some hot-pink tights and black suede ankle boots that used to be my mom's (thanks, Ayumi!), and added a pair of long colorful feather earrings I'd made, and my look was ready. It said, *I'm tough, creative, and independent, and I don't need a crush to make me cool.*

Or maybe it just said, *I like thrift shops.*

Whatever!

When I was going to sleep that night, I gave myself a deadline of twenty-four hours to come up with a cool science project.

## CHAPTER SIX
# CALDER'S CIRCUS

"Have you decided on your science project?" Sierra asked the next morning.

Sierra and I carpooled to school together. Usually my dad drove us to school, and Sierra's mom drove us home. It used to be a three-way car pool with Allie, and we would all squeeze into the back seat. The car pools still felt a little empty without her.

I shrugged. "Not sure yet. I have a few ideas I'm batting around. Something with wire."

"Like a circuit board?" asked Sierra.

"No. Definitely *not* like a circuit board. Something that moves."

"Oh. Like *Calvin's Circus*?"

"What's that?" I asked.

"Hmmm," Sierra answered. "Maybe it wasn't

'Calvin.' Was it 'Cauldron'? Anyway, there was this artist, and he made this whole moving miniature circus out of wire."

"Huh, that actually sounds pretty cool. Where'd you hear about it?"

"I think someone talked about it at a student council meeting. Or maybe it was during a drama club event?" Sierra said. Sierra was involved in so many after-school activities that she could never remember anything.

Just then our car pulled up to the school. Sierra and I parted ways—our lockers were literally across the school from each other.

I pulled out my phone to look up the wire circus. The artist's name was Alexander Calder (not "Calvin" or "Cauldron"). He was an American artist who was famous for his sculptures.

*Calder's Circus* was a big moving wire circus. It used fabric and metal and wood, too, but the basis of all the structures and characters was wire. I found a video that actually showed the artwork in motion. There were wire lion tamers who put their heads inside the mouths of wire lions, there were wire trapeze artists who flipped from one wire trapeze to another, there were wire acrobats who jumped onto the backs of moving wire horses, and somehow, it all looked real! Apparently you could see the actual circus at a museum in New York.

And then it hit me—a wire Felton Pier!

Of course, I wouldn't be able to do the entire Felton Pier in wire (at least not in time for the project due date), but maybe I could do one or two rides, like the Ferris wheel and the merry-go-round. I could bring my idea notebook down there over the weekend on our tasting trip and do lots of sketches, then come home and build the rides out of wire, just like Calder.

And just like that, my science project dilemma was solved. Sierra was a total genius.

Thank youuuu! <3, I texted Sierra.

For what? she texted back. But you're welcome ☺.

Leave it to a BFF to give you inspiration in a time of need!

And leave it to art class to crush a good mood.

"I wish we could switch our partners," I groaned to Sarah, who sat next to me in art class.

"Why? You're with Ewan!" she said. Then she

lowered her voice. "Like, everyone has a crush on him."

"Well, maybe I'm not like everyone else," I grumbled. Seriously, this "everyone has a crush" thing was getting to me. Why was I the only one who didn't like someone?

"You should see Jamie's doodles of Ewan," Sarah continued. "They're seriously good."

"Wait, why is Jamie drawing Ewan? They're not partners."

"Sssshhh, don't talk so loudly!" Sarah hissed, looking around to make sure no one had heard me. "Ewan is Jamie's crush, that's why. Obviously!"

Okay, another thing about this romance stuff that was super-annoying: people thinking that the symptoms of crushes were obvious. It was "obvious" why Jamie was doodling pictures of Ewan. It was "obvious" why Colin was being nice to Allie.

The only thing that was obvious was that I was fed up!

As soon as everyone was in the classroom, Mr. Rivera announced that it was time to find our partners from the week before and pair off again. (I did *not* like how he said "pair off." Ewan and I were *not* a "pair.") I stayed put, and so did Ewan. But this week Mr. Rivera made *me* move to go join Ewan. I thought I could detect a trace of a smirk on Ewan's face as I arrived and dragged a chair next to him, but I didn't study his face for long enough to know for sure. The following week I'd make sure it was Ewan who had to move his seat.

Mr. Rivera began class. "Today we will be sketching posture and attire. Make a note that two weeks from today you will need to wear the same outfit again, so that your partner can add in the colors. Now, for poses let's look at a few samples up on this screen before we get started. Here is an example of a famous pose throughout history. It's a classical pose used by ancient Greeks and Romans called *contrapposto* . . ."

Mr. Rivera's voice droned on. It took some kind of evil skill to make art as boring as Mr. Rivera made it, and I really disliked him for it. Art had always been my favorite class until this year.

I sighed and tuned out. Ewan actually seemed to be paying attention. Humph. Probably trying to think of how to make me look like an ancient Greek.

"I suggest taking turns with your partner today. One person will draw for twenty minutes while the other person poses. Then you will switch," said Mr. Rivera. "Okay, you may begin."

I opened my sketch pad to the page with Ewan's face on it, then turned to a new, fresh sheet to start the full-body portrait. I gave a little bit of an eye roll to show anyone and everyone that I was totally *not* into drawing Ewan.

"Do you want to pose first?" Ewan asked.

I shrugged. "Okay. Have it your way."

I put my sketch pad down and put my hands on my hips as my pose.

Ewan looked up from his pad and smiled. "Seriously?"

"What?" I scoffed.

"Hands on hips? Are you mad about something?"

"No. This is how I sit."

"Even when you're at home, watching TV?"

I raised one eyebrow. "Maybe."

Mr. Rivera arrived just then. He looked over Ewan's shoulder and smiled. "A slow start, Ewan, but I like what you've done so far." Then he turned to me. "How did your memory sketches go over the past week?"

My backpack was at my original table, with my

idea notebook in it. "Oh, I, um, they're in my note-book, back at my table," I said.

"Okay. You can show them to me afterward," said Mr. Rivera. "Next time please keep all of your work in one place." Then he squinted at me. "Ms. Sato! Why are you posing like that? Are you angry at something?"

The classmates close by turned to look at me and laugh. My face grew instantly hot.

"No," I said.

"Then drop your arms. Relax. Chat with your partner."

*Mind your own business!* I wanted to say. But I dropped my arms. Mr. Rivera would have to be happy with that. I was not about to start "chatting" with Ewan.

Instead my mind started to wander. I hadn't real-ized that other people, like Jamie, were jealous that Ewan was my partner. I remembered what Sierra had said on video chat about crushes. It meant thinking that someone was cute and wanting to go on a date. So people actually felt that way about Ewan?

I tried to imagine myself going on a date with Ewan: smiling, holding hands, and sharing an ice cream sundae together at Molly's. Ewwww! I flailed my arms, trying to swat the image out of my mind.

"I can't draw if you keep moving!" Evan complained.

I resumed my pose but let my eyes wander around the classroom. I tried to imagine myself going on a date with every single classmate. By the time I was finished going through everyone in the room, I had held twenty-eight hands and eaten twenty-eight imaginary sundaes. But nobody had clicked. I hadn't felt my heart fluttering, or my palms sweating, or whatever "obvious" symptoms I was supposed to feel.

"Uh, Tamiko?" Ewan said, snapping me back to reality. "Can you stop looking around? Your pose keeps changing, and it's really annoying."

I sighed loudly. My arms were starting to cramp from staying still.

"Ten more minutes!" Mr. Rivera called. "Then you'll switch with your partner."

When would this class ever end?

## CHAPTER SEVEN
# FELTON PIER, MY DEAR

"Felton Pier, Felton Pier, here I come, oh my dear!"
I sang at the top of my lungs on Saturday morning.
I was getting dressed for our outing, and I wanted to
go with a fun, colorful look today. I layered a pink
pullover vest with a white long-sleeved shirt. Then
I added my pink-and-white checkered pants. Of
course, I still needed accessories: multicolored hair-
pins; a purple bracelet and a matching ring; and my
new graffiti Keds, now painted. I stood in front of the
mirror and examined my outfit. It was perfect!

I could not wait to head out with my besties. It
was an unseasonably warm Saturday—sunny, with
big puffy clouds.

After doing a bunch of homework, I packed a

little drawstring knapsack with a sweater, my wallet, my idea notebook (because *flavor notes!* And also: *Felton Pier drawings for science!*), and my Hello Kitty pencil case filled with pens and pencils.

At eleven forty I hopped into my mom's giant white van, and we cruised over to Molly's to meet my friends.

"How is your homework situation, Tamiko?" my mom asked.

"Almost done, Ayumi!" I chirped.

"Don't call me Ayumi. What does 'almost done' really mean? *Really* almost done or, 'Oh, I forgot I have this huge project due and it's ten o'clock on Sunday night'?"

"Calm down, Ayumi," I said, and grinned. My mom hated it when I told her to calm down, but she knew I was joking.

"Pfft!" She swatted at the air between us.

"It means I still have my math worksheet to do, and yes, I do have a big science project due in a week, but I'm on it. I can't do it until after Felton Pier anyway."

We stopped at a signal light, and she gave me a quick death stare. "What is this big project?"

"I'm doing Felton Pier in wire for my physics project. Like *Calder's Circus*," I said breezily. I figured she wouldn't know what that was and I'd be in the clear.

I figured wrong.

"Tamiko! *Calder's Circus*! Are you crazy? That's going to be a huge project. It could take months to render Felton Pier in wire!"

"Well," I huffed, "I'm only doing a few rides. Or maybe just one." I looked out the window. "We'll see how it goes."

"Yes, we sure will. Tomorrow morning, bright and early!"

"Ugh, Mommy!" I cried.

"Don't 'Ugh, Mommy' me, young lady. I know how you are. You get all obsessive with your projects and they have to be detailed and perfect."

I rolled my eyes. "I wonder where I get that from!"

"Tsk. So fresh! Here we are."

My mom eased the car up in front of Molly's, and I popped out before she'd even come to a complete stop.

"Tamiko Sato! Don't run away from me, young lady!"

I turned back. "What?" I said, deliberately standing five feet from the car window.

"Come." She waved me in, and I shuffled a few steps toward her. "Do you need money?" she asked.

"Nope!" I grinned and patted my rucksack. "I'm a working woman now, remember? Plus Mrs. S. is giving us a food allowance."

"That's very generous of her. Make sure you are very polite and use your best manners. Daddy and I have to go to the Grahams' for dinner tonight, so Kai will pick you up afterward if you text him when you get close."

I saluted her. "Roger, Ayumi!" I cried, and I scurried away as "Don't call me Ayumi!" floated behind me on the breeze.

Dashing into Molly's, I dodged a couple of customers and headed behind the counter.

"Hi, Mrs. S.!" I greeted Allie's mom. "Need help with anything?"

"Hi, Tamiko! I'm all set, honey. The girls are in the office waiting for Allie's dad. Why don't you head on back?"

She didn't need to tell me twice. In the office Allie and Sierra were huddled over Allie's phone.

"Miko!" cried Allie when I appeared. We all squealed as I chanted, "Felton Pier, Felton Pier, here we come, oh my dear!"

"I love your outfit, Miko!" said Sierra. "And your shoes!"

"Thanks. I went all out on the pink today."

"Nailed it," said Sierra admiringly.

"We were just looking at Colin's SuperSnap." Allie smiled sheepishly.

"Just doing a little cyber-spying," joked Sierra.

"Wow, sounds fun," I said in a flat voice, 'cause it *didn't*!

Allie and Sierra might have exchanged a tiny look just then, but I didn't press it. It would not pay to get into a fight right before we were spending the day together, so I let it go.

"Are we going to do all the rides today?" I asked, changing the subject.

"Totally!" said Allie.

"Uh-huh." Sierra fist-bumped us.

"Excellent."

"Girls!" We heard Mr. S. calling us from the front of the store, and we quickly gathered our things and scurried up front.

"Bye, Mrs. S.! Thanks for sending us on this important business trip!" I said as we hustled out to Allie's dad's car.

She just laughed and waved. "Have fun, Sprinkle Sundays sisters!"

We chatted the whole way to Felton Pier. With the three of us squeezed into the back seat, it felt just like the car pools we used to have. Except today we weren't going to school—we were going to Felton Pier!

Mr. S. told us funny stories about Allie and Tanner, her little brother. He told us one really good one about Allie stuffing her face with chicken nuggets and then going on the Salt 'n' Pepper Shakers ride and throwing up all over the people below.

"Dad!" Allie shrieked while he was telling the story, but he wouldn't stop.

"I tell it from a place of love, Al," he said.

"You tell it from a place of puke!" she cried. Then she covered her ears and sang "Lalala" until it was over. Sierra and I loved the story.

"I'll make sure to warn Colin if he ever takes you to Felton Pier," said Sierra, elbowing Allie.

"And who is this Colin you speak of?" said Allie's dad in a fake-newscaster voice.

"Just a friend in my class," said Allie, rolling her eyes at Sierra.

Sierra grinned. "And maybe a cruuuuush!" she sing-songed.

"You girls are too young for crushes!" said Mr. S.

"That's what I think, Mr. S.!" I said.

"No, we're not!" said Allie and Sierra in unison.

Who did *Sierra* like? I'd never heard her mention anyone beyond movie stars. This stupid crush thing was like a virus. Everyone who caught it turned into some kind of zombie!

"Well, put that all on hold today," said Mr. S. "Saturdays are for the girls!"

"And Sundays!" I added. "We're the Sprinkle Sundays sisters, after all."

"*Every* day is BFF day," Sierra said.

I glanced over at Allie. For Allie every day was a "different parent" day. Some days she was with her dad, and some days she was with her mom. Even if I wasn't part of the Shear family (or was it now two families?), it felt weird to me. I made a mental note to ask Sierra sometime if she was still getting used to the divorce too.

When we got to Felton Pier, Mr. Shear parked the car and we strolled into the park. We bought strips of ride and game tickets from the little kiosk at the entrance, but we had other things in store first.

"In the *mood* for *food!*" I said, and the others agreed.

"Let's go, moody foodies," said Allie, linking arms with us.

We made a circuit of all the options, paying special attention to what little kids and their parents were eating. Then we set about trying each and every item. Mr. S. took himself over to a bench in the sunshine and said he'd move when we were ready for rides.

First stop was the Fry-o-Lator. That was the stand where they fried everything, and I mean *everything*. There were fried green tomatoes (bitter), fried pickles (sour and salty), fried alligator tail, fried chicken strips and nuggets, french fries, and homemade potato chips. Then came the fried desserts: fried Twinkies, fried Oreos, fried cookie dough, and my favorite— fried Snickers bars. We got the sampler platter, which had a little of everything, including a funnel cake, half a fried Twinkie, and half a fried Snickers. It was a good start.

I whipped out my notebook and kept track of everything we tried, how much we liked it, and—most important—whether it would make a good ice cream flavor. My hand could hardly move fast enough as I jotted down all our thoughts and tips. Yes to fried Twinkie with a vanilla custard–based ice cream, and yes to funnel cake in cinnamon ice cream. Allie and Sierra gave a definite no to the fried alligator! Texture was as big a factor as taste for all of us. We had to think in terms of ice cream. If something was too gloppy before it went into ice cream, it would totally fall apart once it got "wet."

Our next stop was the Juicery. Here we tried small sips of watermelon juice (kind of watery), homemade grape juice (sour), peach juice (really, really good, but not that original for an ice cream flavor), and sour cherry juice (starred—tart and a great color). Fruit flavors were a breeze for Mrs. S., and they weren't too expensive since a little fruit extract and puree went a long way. The sour cherry and peach were must-trys, maybe even mixed together.

We waved at Mr. Shear on his reading bench after the Juicery and moved on to Skinny Dippers. This was a stand that hand-dipped fruit into various toppings, made to order. We got a frozen banana dipped in chocolate and then rolled in crushed peanuts, like an inside-out banana split (hold the ice cream).

"Yum!" I said.

"Banana Split would be a great flavor, even if it is obvious!" said Sierra, and we all agreed.

"You can't beat a classic," I said.

"I want to try a candy apple!" said Allie. "I love those, and I haven't had one in years!"

"They are so good, but they really wouldn't make a good ice cream flavor, you know? The red shellac would be too hard when it froze. You'd chip your tooth!" (I sounded like my mom, which made me shudder.) "I mean, I don't want to be a downer, but ..."

"No, you're right. We're here for work. We have a mission!" Allie replied.

"Our mission is to *improve* the ice cream *condition!*" I said, all dramatic, like a superhero. This made us laugh like crazy. When Allie decided to order a toffee apple instead, dipped in warm, soft caramel, Sierra and I chanted, "On a *mission!* On a *mission!*" as she placed her order. The college kid working behind the counter gave us all a weird look, but we found it hilarious.

"Mmm, mmm, mmm! This is so good, you guys! You have to try it!" Allie held the gooey treat toward us for bites. It was a little hard to eat and kind of unsanitary. You'd go for a bite, and once you had the caramel in your mouth, it was hard to get a bite of the apple, too. Then the caramel would all start to pull away from the apple and you'd have to hold it in place while you completed your bite.

But it *was* insanely good.

"Wow!" I said when I had unclogged my throat from the caramel. "That is something we could definitely work with, *amiright*?"

"Yes, totally. Maybe tart green apple ice cream with a dulce de leche caramel ribbon?" said Allie thoughtfully.

"*Ribbon?* I'm thinking more like a caramel rope, sister!" I said.

"Yeah, a thick caramel *cable*!" agreed Sierra.

I made some more flavor notes in the idea book and drew stars all around the caramel apple concept, with our specs about tart green apple, thick caramel, and maybe even chunks of fresh apple on top.

"Okay, that was sugar. Now we need something savory again," said Sierra.

"Meat Treats?" Sierra suggested, squinting at a stand that had smoke billowing from its grill.

"Th-that is the *worst* name!" Allie sputtered.

"The Dog House?" suggested Sierra.

"I'll go anywhere," I said. "Remember—follow the crowds."

The Dog House had a huge line with kids, so we checked out their offerings next.

"Corn Dog Ripple?" said Allie with a sly grin.

"I'm thinking Bratwurst Brickle!" I said.

"Tube Steak Twirl?" offered Sierra.

"Pass!" I said. "Okay, so not all the popular foods will make good ice cream flavors. Meat Treats?" We strolled over.

"Steak on a Stick Chip?" Allie said, and then giggled.

"Keep walking!" I intoned.

"'Spaghetti Donuts'?" Sierra read the sign aloud.

"On a mission, on a mission," I chanted.

"On a mission, on a mission," agreed the others.

"Nuts about Nuts?" said Allie, coming to an abrupt halt. Sierra and I plowed into her and stopped too.

"Yes. And your mom does have that whole ice

cream case segregated for nut ice creams, so we have the space to do a couple more," said Sierra.

I pulled out the notebook and began scribbling as the ideas flew out of us: Pistachio Cream. Peanut Butter Fudge. Cashew Butter. PB&J. Nuts about Nuts, with every nut. Nutter Butter, with cookies and peanut butter. Turtle, with caramel and pecans and dark chocolate . . . and so on. We came up with ten nut flavors alone!

"I *am* nuts about nut ice cream flavors. I wouldn't have thought it, but it's true," I said.

"Ooh! Look! Frozen lemonade!" said Sierra. "Love!"

I wrote that down too. "And frozen pineapple," I agreed, looking at the other slushy flavors at the Ice Shack.

Walking farther, we found Mellow Mallow, where everything was marshmallow and there was a crowd of little kids gathered—the biggest crowd we'd seen so far. There were Rice Krispies Treats galore—some dipped in chocolate and studded with different kinds of candy and sprinkles, M&M's Minis and chocolate chips, and more. Some treats were dipped in caramel and decorated with candy flowers or micro-mini marshmallows. Then there were plain marshmallows dipped in chocolate or caramel; marshmallow kebabs, alternating on a stick with jelly candies; big sheets of marshmallow, like blankets of pillowy fudge; hot chocolate with marshmallows . . .

"Hey! See!" said Sierra. "Hot chocolate. And it's popular with the kids."

"I like how they use those tiny mini-marshies in the hot chocolate," I agreed. "They're almost like marshmallow sprinkles. Cute."

"Just sayin'," said Sierra with a shrug.

"I'm writing it down. Maybe we rotate out the Rocky Road for a while and rotate in the Hot Chocolate," I suggested.

Carrying some marshmallow treats, a frozen lemonade, a tub of kettle corn (I put it on the list too!), and three slices of pizza (not a potential ice cream flavor but a necessity for lunch), we struggled over to where Mr. S. was sitting, to take a chow break and rest. The Keds were kind of pinching my feet. I'd gone for style over comfort in my footwear, and I was regretting it already. I made a mental note to self: *Fancy Keds are for show, not play.*

"How's it going so far?" asked Allie's dad, helping himself to a big handful of kettle corn.

"Great!" I enthused. Balancing my pizza slice on my knee, I flipped through the three pages of ideas and comments I'd jotted down already.

"We even kept a list of rejects," I added.

"Let's hear those," said Mr. S., laughing.

I read the list. "Fried green tomato, corn dog, steak chip—"

"Stop! Gross!" cried Sierra. "Read the good ones."

"Frozen Lemonade, Hot Chocolate Marshmallow, Pistachio Cream, PB&J . . ." On and on I went, reading the list. We had about twenty-five flavors so far, most of them really good and doable.

"Wow," said Mr. S. "I'm impressed."

"We don't fool around!" said Allie.

"We're on a *mission*!" I added, and we all laughed like crazy, leaving Mr. S. looking perplexed.

We had bought so much food that we could barely eat it all. Most of the kettle corn ended up going to Mr. S. After our lunch, we all sank down into the bench.

"I feel like I ate a year's worth of junk food," Allie moaned.

"I just want to crawl into my bed and take a nap," Sierra groaned.

I patted my stomach in agreement. A nap sounded like a good idea. Then I clapped my hand over my mouth and jumped up. "We forgot something really, really important!"

"What?" asked Allie, her eyes wide.

"Rides!"

## CHAPTER EIGHT
# THRILLS & CHILLS

My favorite ride was the Tilt-A-Whirl, and we did it first. Sure, we were the biggest kids on it by far, and some of the little kids gave us puzzled looks while we waited in line, but Sierra, Allie, and I loved it! It was a good start to ease us into the rides, and Mr. S. snapped a great photo of us in the candy-apple-red car when we spun past him, our mouths open wide as we screamed in delight.

I didn't think the Tilt-A-Whirl would be easy to re-create in wire, though. I started a fresh page in my notebook and drew a line down the middle, then wrote at the top of the columns: "Good Wire Rides" and "Bad Wire Rides." After each ride I wrote it in the proper column.

"Let's do the carousel!" cheered Allie when we stumbled off the Tilt-A-Whirl. In total agreement, the three of us jogged over to the ride and stood in the short line, again towering over the other kids.

"People are going to think we're weirdos," said Sierra, but she was laughing.

"Who cares? We're reliving our childhoods!" I replied.

"And it feels good!" said Allie.

We did a three-way hug and shuffled forward to get on the ride.

The most fun part about this carousel was that it went fast. You really felt like you were whipping past the spectators in a real horse race. Mr. S.'s face was a blur as we sailed by, waving each time in the vague direction of where he stood.

Sierra managed to grab the brass ring and got an extra ride for it. Allie and I stood alongside the ride and waved and cheered like crazy whenever she passed us. We were so into it, with each of us trying to outdo the other in wildness every time she passed, that Mr. S. stepped a few paces away from us, saying he didn't want people to know we were with him. This just made us act crazier and tease him, saying,

"Don't pretend you're not with us!" until he turned red with embarrassment.

When Sierra came off, she was super-dizzy, so we had to take a little break while she steadied her brain. Then we hit the bumper cars.

The bumper cars were a true delight for me. I was a maniac driver, and I lived to smash into strangers. Allie and Sierra wanted to just cruise around the track and avoid everyone, but I aimed right for them and barreled full steam ahead.

"Oh no! Here she comes!" Sierra would scream.

I'd cackle like a wicked villain and say, "I'll get you, my pretties!" Then I'd slam into them as they yelled, "Stop! Truce! You win!"

I even slammed into some dad, who looked at me like I was nuts and accidentally smashed into two younger kids.

"Sorry!" I called as I reversed away from the scene of the crime.

When the power to the cars suddenly cut off, I felt weak and exposed—I had to get out of there before someone came after me for revenge!

"Let's run, girls!" I screamed, and Allie and Sierra chased after me, all of us laughing and wild.

Unfortunately, bumper cars had to go on the list of Bad Wire Rides. I would have had to make way too many identical cars for it to work.

The swings were awesome because they lifted us kind of high and we could catch glimpses of the ocean as we spun.

The swings went on the Good Wire Rides list with a star next to it. That would be a great one. I took a minute to sketch the ride when we got off, estimating the size and ratio of all the main parts. It would be pretty easy to do. I'd just need something solid to form the central base and the roof. Then I could make the individual swings out of wire and hang them off the roof. It would have to spin, obviously. But it was definitely doable. If I painted the roof with red and white stripes, it would look like something out of *Calder's Circus*.

Next we went on the roller coaster. The term "roller coaster" might make people think of a huge ride with giant hills. This was more of a kiddie coaster (we could barely fold our knees into the small cars), and it was fast, though not scary. It would have made a Good Wire Ride, but even I had to admit, it was maybe too complicated for me to build.

The Salt 'n' Pepper Shakers were a highlight. Sierra and I screamed the whole time, "Look out below!" and laughed like crazy. Allie did look a little green when we got off, but she held it together and recovered after drinking a Coke. (Cola-flavored ice cream went on the list then, as did root beer and lemon-lime fizz.)

We worked our way through all the rides we could fit on. (Some of them, we had to admit, were just too babyish for us, like the little helicopters that went in a slow circle and lifted four feet off the ground, then came gently back down, only to lift again.) The Round Up went on the Good Wire Rides list with ten stars next to it. It was a ride where you stood on the inside of a huge circular platform with a wall along the outside edge. When the platform started spinning, the centrifugal force pushed you against the wall. The force was so strong that you couldn't peel yourself off the wall even if you tried!

But no other rides made the cut until the Ferris wheel.

"Do we want a stationary car, or one that swings?" asked Allie, looking at the two different lines you could stand in. The swinging-car line was longer, but there was really no contest.

"Duh!" I said, barreling toward the swinging-car line.

The line took us right under the wheel, which was tall, tall, tall. I craned my neck to look up at all the iron bars crisscrossing one another to hold up the Ferris wheel. It was definitely a Good Wire Ride, but now that I looked at it up close, I wasn't sure I'd have the time to build it.

We inched along until finally we were up next. Our car swung down into position, and as the people exited it on the other side, we hopped in and swung right up and out.

We sat on the bench all together and held hands, screaming as we lifted into the air. We were kind of hamming it up—we weren't moving that fast—but it was faster than I remembered and kind of shaky.

As we lifted high, high above Felton Pier, the view opened up and we could see way out to sea. The air was cold and damp and salty, and the sunshine bright and sharp.

"Wow!" I breathed. "I can see the whole world from here!"

Sierra shook her head. "I can't look! I'm afraid of heights!"

"What?" I laughed. "How do I not know this about you?"

Sierra squeezed her eyes closed. "We never go anywhere up high together! Now you know!"

"Colin's scared of heights too. When I told him we were coming here—he asked me to do an article about it, by the way—he said we were taking our lives in our hands, riding these rickety old rides." Allie grimaced.

I raised my eyebrows, annoyed. "Colin's clueless. These rides aren't ricket—*Oh!*" I screamed as our car swung out on its track as we rounded the top of the wheel. It felt like we were going to go shooting right off the side of the ride and go flinging out into the ocean. We screamed for real, at the tops of our lungs, closing our eyes and clutching one another. When the car stabilized, we all laughed hysterically, but it had been scary.

"See?" said Sierra. "And you guys thought I was crazy!"

"I forgot how scary the swinging cars are! That was awesome! I want to do it again!" I said.

"You're nuts!" cried Allie.

I tuned out and enjoyed the view for a minute. It was really breathtaking, and from the top you could see all up and down the coast for miles and miles. It made my irritation with all these recent crushes seem sort of petty.

"Should we try some games after this?" I asked.

"Yes, I want to be on firm ground for a while after—Aaaaaah!" shrieked Sierra as our car swung out again to the edge of the wheel. I laughed like crazy and kept my eyes open this time.

"Bring it on!" I yelled. I was ready for whatever came at me.

Most of the carnival games were rigged so that we wouldn't win. Even though we knew that, we tried to throw rubber rings onto old Coke bottles, but they all bounced off. We sprayed water into clowns' mouths, and Allie won a tiny stuffed monkey. We threw softballs at pyramids of other softballs, and I won an inflatable plastic beach ball that was cute and matched my outfit perfectly.

Mr. S. wanted to be sure Sierra won something, so we went to an easy game where you threw a fishing line over a fence and the magnet on it picked up some junky thing on the other side. Sierra won a little plastic purse that she thought was adorable.

After a while we were ready to wrap things up. All the sugar had worn off, so we were tired, and it was getting chilly.

"Are you kids ready to head home?" asked Mr. S. I think he certainly was, but he'd had fun with us, I knew. "One last game?" he asked as we passed El Toro Loco.

"Haha, Mr. S.," I said. "That game's impossible. No one wins! You can tell by the prizes!"

The only prizes were giant—and I mean GIANT—stuffed bulls hanging overhead. They were around five feet long and three feet high, with huge felt horns and brown shaggy coats.

Mr. S. laughed. "You're right. But we might as well use up our last tickets if we have any?"

We all searched our pockets and came up with seven tickets. The game cost six.

"Let's do it!" he said, walking up to the counter. The game was a simple basketball toss, but you only got one ball. It didn't look that hard, but it must've been rigged somehow, because no one was stopping there to even try.

"Who wants to do it?" asked Allie's dad.

"No, thanks," said Allie. "Too much pressure!"

Sierra shook her head. "Me neither. How about Tamiko?"

I shrugged. "It's totally rigged. There's no way I'll win. Maybe you should do it, Mr. S."

But Allie's dad shook his head and put the tickets down on the counter. The carnival kid handed him a basketball, and he held it out to me. "Go for it," he said.

I took a deep breath and focused. I held the ball in one hand and mimed throwing it a few times, just to get the feel of it.

"Come on, Tamiko!" said Allie.

"You can do it, *chica*!" cheered Sierra.

I bounced the ball once or twice, just to ham it up and get our money's worth. Then I lifted the ball into the air, and . . . *swoosh!* It went right into the basket!

"What?" I screamed, turning to my friends in shock. "I won!" We grabbed one another and jumped up and down as a unit, yelling and cheering.

Even the carnival kid was shocked. "I've never seen anyone win before!" he said. "I don't even know how to get the bull down for you!"

He had to call a supervisor and have the lady

come over with a stick to lift the giant prize down for me. She let me pick the one I wanted, and I chose the bull with a kind of smushy-looking pug face.

Mr. S. said, "Let me go pull the car up to the entrance so we don't have to lug that thing all the way though the parking lot."

As he walked off to the car, I hugged Allie around her neck and said, "Your dad is the best."

She looked at me and smiled. "He is pretty great, isn't he?"

Sierra nodded. "He's that good kind of dad who makes things more fun but isn't annoyingly in the middle of everything, taking over."

"Totally," I agreed. "*And* he thinks we're funny."

Allie glowed happily. "It's true."

"This was the best day ever!" I crowed. "And I can't believe I won El Toro!"

"OMG, where is he going to sit in the car?" Sierra said, and laughed.

"We might have to strap him to the roof!" said Allie.

The car ride back to Bayville was quieter. Sierra fell asleep, and Mr. S. listened to the radio, so we didn't talk. El Toro was smashed into the cargo area in the back. He was already leaking some tiny Styrofoam pellets. I'd have to sew up his seam when I got home.

I pulled out my notebook and looked over my ice cream notes with satisfaction. Mrs. S. had definitely gotten her money's worth today. We had a good list of ideas and a side list of market research—of which stands had the longest lines, and which foods the little kids ate the most of. (Fact: they preferred the sweetest flavors over anything else, which was a little boring but true.)

Next I reviewed my list of rides and the sketches I'd done of them. I was definitely thinking I'd do the swings for my project. They illustrated motion and speed and centrifugal force and weren't as hard to build as a Ferris wheel. I added a few more details to my sketch—estimating the length of the chains on the swings and the size of the swing seats relative to the ride. These were really good notes that would help me when I started my project.

As we reached the outskirts of Bayville, I texted Kai to let him know I was almost there and asked him to come get me. He texted me back one letter, *K*, and I put my phone away in my rucksack.

As we pulled up outside Molly's Ice Cream, I could see that it was hopping. Lots of people were going in and out, and it made me feel good.

"We might have to help mom!" Allie said to her dad, peering out the car window.

"I'll park, and we can go in and check. But first let's help Tamiko with El Toro," said Mr. S.

Mr. S. popped open the tailgate as we climbed out of the car.

"Poor El Toro!" I cried. The stuffed bull was all squished.

"Where can we put him?" asked Mr. S.

I looked around, but Kai hadn't arrived yet. "How about if I just wait out here on the bench?" I suggested. "Assuming Mrs. S. doesn't need my help in the store."

"I'll run in and check," said Sierra. "Be right back."

Mr. S. helped me carry El Toro to the bench as Allie closed the tailgate. Mr. S. was laughing. "Your parents are going to kill me for letting you bring this thing home! Where are you going to put him?" he asked.

"In my room! He'll be like a beanbag chair. I can sit on him."

Mr. S. laughed again. "I knew you'd have a plan, Tamiko!"

"Thanks!"

Mr. S. settled El Toro on the bench as if the bull were a customer. I sat down next to him. Then four things happened all at once:

Sierra popped out to say that she and Allie would help Mrs. S. with the store, so I was free to take El Toro home.

Kai pulled up in front of the store to pick me up.

Allie jumped out of her dad's car holding my notebook, which I'd left behind.

And Ewan and his friends Jake and Connor came walking up and said hi to me as they entered Molly's. Ewan's eyes grew huge when he saw El Toro, so I hustled into Kai's car because I was so embarrassed.

And with all those distractions, plus wedging El Toro into the car, that was how I left my idea notebook on the bench.

## CHAPTER NINE
# BOOKLESS

It wasn't until I'd gotten home, settled El Toro into a corner of my room, showered, and gotten into my cozy sweats that I realized the notebook was missing.

"Shoot!" I said as I punched the contact for Molly's on my phone. I knew exactly where I'd left it—on the bench outside the store. After my graceless exit with El Toro in front of Ewan, I'd just wanted to peel out of there ASAP, and I'd forgotten to go back and get it.

"Molly's Ice Cream. Allie speaking," said Allie when she picked up on the other end.

"Ali-li! Thanks for an amazing day!" I cried into the phone.

"It was super-fun, wasn't it?" she agreed.

"Totes. Listen. If you can please bring my note-book home with you, I'll stop by first thing tomorrow to pick it up, okay? Are you at your mom's or dad's tonight?"

"Wait, what?"

"My notebook. I left it on the bench outside the store. Someone must've brought it inside, right?" Suddenly my hands felt icy. "Right?"

"Um, I'm not sure. Hang on." Allie put her hand over the phone receiver, but I could still hear her asking everyone. She got back on. "No one brought it in. Let me run and get it. It's probably still on the bench. Hang on again, okay?"

"Yup," I said. "Thanks." I could picture the note-book sitting on the bench, and I thanked my lucky stars that it wasn't raining out, or that thing would have been totally ruined. I looked at my fingernails as I waited. Maybe I'd do a fun manicure after this. Something carnival-themed.

"Miko?" said Allie.

"Got it?"

"Um . . . no. It wasn't there. I'm so sorry!"

"Wait, what?" My stomach dropped, even worse than on the swinging Ferris wheel car. "Are you sure you looked really carefully? Like, behind the bench, or maybe someone put it on the window ledge. . . ."

"Tamiko, I'm so sorry. I really looked all over. Even in the tree bed by the curb and on top of the fire hydrant and all around. It's . . . gone."

"Oh no." I sat down heavily on El Toro. "What am I going to do?"

I could feel the tears welling up in my eyes. Allie assured me that they'd keep looking and that some customer must've picked it up and surely it would be returned any minute.

I didn't have a lot of confidence in that outcome. After I hung up with Allie, I started mentally reviewing all the project ideas I had in that book, not to mention all my best carnival stickers that I'd used on the cover. There was all our ice cream research— which Mrs. S. had paid for—and losing that made me an irresponsible employee. And of course all my info for the science project was in there: the sketches, the dimension estimates, the ratios, the scientific concepts. All missing.

And worst of all, of course, were the pages and pages of drawings of Ewan Kim. I cringed, thinking of kids flipping through and laughing. They'd probably assume I was doodling pictures of my crush, since I had recently learned that drawing someone was an "obvious" indication that you liked them.

I ran down the stairs. "Kai! Kai!"

"In here!" he called from the TV room, where he was doing his homework. "What's the matter? You sound frantic, dude."

"That's because I am frantic. Can you please, please give me a ride back to Molly's? I lost something and just have to go check for myself that it's not there."

"Seriously, Tamiko? I just got all settled in to write a draft of my midterm paper for AP Economics. Do we really need to go right now?"

My eyes welled up. "Yes."

Kai looked at me and sighed heavily. "Fine." He wasn't happy about it, but he stood up and walked to the front hall, where he grabbed his car keys and jammed his feet into his Allbirds sneakers. "Let's go."

I was quiet in the car, thinking of all the wrong hands my notebook could have fallen into. A toddler who got the pages all sticky. A busy mom who spilled her coffee milkshake onto it. Some slob who tore out pages and used them to blow his nose. A terrible thought occurred to me. *What if someone who knew Ewan had found it?* Oh no! They'd probably show him the pictures, and they'd all think I was in love with him and would have a huge belly laugh at my expense.

I put my hands over my eyes.

"Are you okay?" asked Kai.

Sighing, I shook my head. "There was a lot of stuff in that notebook that I need."

Kai bit his lip. "Anything I can help you with?"

"No." I shook my head. "But thanks," I added.

Outside Molly's, I looked everywhere for the notebook. It was hard to look for something at dusk, and I had to use the flashlight on my phone to see. I checked under the bench, on the sidewalk. I even peeked inside the trash can to see if someone had thrown it away. Mrs. S. was the only person inside the store. I didn't want her to see me, or I'd have to confess that I'd lost all our research.

Allie was right, though. The notebook wasn't there.

Back in the car, Kai offered to take me to Sushirrito, one of my favorite restaurants, where they serve a mash-up of sushi and burritos. But after all the junk I'd had at Felton Pier, and thinking about my current tragedy, I declined. We went home and had salads from the fridge, and I did not give myself a carnival-themed manicure. Instead I tried to finish my math worksheet, but I kept getting distracted.

I pulled out my phone and sent a text in the group chat I shared with Allie and Sierra. Any good news?

Allie wrote back right away. No, sorry ☹. No one dropped off your notebook.

What happened? Did you lose your notebook? Sierra chimed in.

I filled Sierra in on the situation. She was super-nice about it and didn't get mad. Still, I felt terrible about losing all of our hard work.

I also told them about losing the science project info, but not about the sketches of Ewan. The last thing I wanted right now was for my besties to think I had a crush on him.

Losing my notebook was the worst ending to an otherwise amazing day. I tried to remember all the good things that had happened: the delicious food, the fun rides, the prizes I'd won. But all my thoughts ended up on the lost notebook. I went to sleep early, my pillow damp with tears.

The next morning I woke up early and started a huge internet search for the details and specifications of carnival swing rides. When I took a break, my mom asked how my homework was going, and I explained that it was hard to re-create the project without my notes. She offered to drive me back to Felton Pier, but I declined. I had to be at work by twelve forty-five, and there just wasn't enough time for it to be worthwhile. My mom wondered aloud if I could miss a day of work, since it was for academic reasons, but I imagined my friends' faces if I'd canceled, and I just couldn't do it. They'd think I was avoiding work because I'd lost our research.

I hugged her hard anyway.

"Thanks, Mama," I said. No "Ayumi" this time. I wasn't in the mood to tease her when she was being so nice to me.

I trudged back upstairs to keep googling and to work on some mock-ups. It was tough because I really needed an extra pair of hands to hold things in place while I added the central supports. I didn't want to ask my parents for help quite yet. In the past they had just taken over and gotten all bossy and annoying.

While I worked, I kept a blank sheet of paper next to me and tried to remember our flavor research. Each time something popped into my head, I wrote it down. Frozen Lemonade. Hot Chocolate Marshmallow. Cola. I had an easier time remembering the ones we'd come up with first and last, but all the stuff in the middle—when we'd really been jamming— was kind of a muddle.

My phone pinged with a text, and I dove for it, expecting to see a text from Allie saying that someone had turned in my idea notebook at the store.

Instead it was a text from my friend Keiko, who used to go to Japanese school with me. She and our other good friend Ken had basically become boyfriend-girlfriend, kind of behind my back, and it really bugged me. It wrecked our whole friendship trio.

The text said, Miko! Ken hasn't texted me in three days! Do you think he doesn't like me anymore? ☹

"ARRRGGHH!" I yelled.

*How the heck would I know what Ken is thinking? If I were psychic, I'd know where my notebook is!*

After an hour of brainstorming for my science project, my craft table looked like a war zone.

There were half-built swings and balled-up chunks of cardboard, and little tubs of clay and paint open everywhere. I was stumped. I cleaned up a little, then had some lunch and got ready to go to work.

My feet dragged as I slunk toward Molly's. If I'd been a dog, I would have had my tail between my legs. I dreaded facing Mrs. S. and telling her I'd carelessly lost all our valuable research.

Inside, Allie was there, and she didn't say anything. Just came and gave me a huge hug.

Sierra showed up soon after and did the same. Then Sierra said, "Let's make a list of all the flavors we can remember, okay? It'll be kind of fun! Like a memory game!"

Half-heartedly I accepted a piece of paper and a pen from her, and we began naming everything we could think of. I wrote:

- Cola
- Frozen Lemonade
- Bratwurst Brickle! (Haha)
- Pistachio Cream
- Fried Pickle

And so on, until we had seventeen flavors listed.

"Guys! That's not too bad!" said Sierra.

"Not at all," said Allie. "And maybe the other flavors will come to us. The most important ones were Hot Chocolate Marshmallow—because that drew a crowd—and Caramel Apple. But what were the details for Caramel Apple again?"

"A huge cable of caramel!" crowed Sierra.

"And chopped green apple on top. I can remember that!" I said. "Group hug, besties! Thanks for helping me to remember. I'll keep thinking of the others."

"You know what they say! Three heads are better than one!" said Sierra.

"So true," I agreed. "Now, should we edit down the list to just our recommendations, or leave everything on it?"

"Let's leave it all," Sierra said. "Then Allie's mom will know how hard we worked."

"If that was hard work, sign me up to be the CEO!" Allie said, laughing.

"Should we wait to present it next week, when we've had some more time? And maybe the notebook will have turned up?" suggested Sierra.

Allie nodded. "Sure. I don't think my mom minds either way. She's got a pretty good stockpile of flavors in the deep freeze for now."

My phone pinged, and because there were no customers in the store and because I was still hoping someone would return my notebook, I took a peek.

It was Keiko again. Miko! What should I do? Dying for your advice!

"Grrr!" I growled, and I shoved the phone back into my pocket.

"What's wrong?" asked Allie.

I unloaded on them about Keiko and Ken, and how annoying it was that people kept asking me for advice when the last thing I wanted to be talking about was romance.

"Well, maybe Keiko's asking not because she thinks you're a love expert but just because you're her friend," Allie said. "I kind of get it. I like asking for your opinion a lot too."

"What do you mean?" I asked.

"Well," Allie answered, "if I wanted advice about anything, I would go to you. It's not because I think you're a fortune-teller but because you wouldn't sugar-coat anything or just tell me what I want to hear. I always know you'll give me a straight, honest answer."

"Even though it can be harsh sometimes!" Sierra said, laughing.

"You too, Sierra." Allie smiled. "I'm happy that I can talk about anything with my besties."

Sierra pulled us into a group hug. It felt nice, but the fuzzy feeling disappeared once I pulled away. Allie's words didn't really solve my problems. What was I supposed to say to Keiko? "I'm sick of hearing about people's crushes that I don't care about, and I wish you would stop being so love crazy about Ken"? That was way too rude to say, even if I were giving a straight and honest answer.

I sighed, quietly enough that my Sprinkle Sundays sisters wouldn't hear.

## CHAPTER TEN
# LIONHEARTED WARRIOR

I tried to go to bed early again on Sunday night, but I couldn't fall asleep. Lying in bed, I thought of where my idea notebook might be and cringed to think of someone looking inside. What if some rival ice cream shop owner found the list of flavors and stole our amazing ideas? I couldn't believe I had been so careless with top secret market research.

Then I thought again about someone seeing my art homework sketches. They'd surely think I had a thing for Ewan. Why else would I be doodling pictures of him? If I ever got it back, it would be hard to explain to the person—without me seeming weird and a little desperate—that the Ewan drawings were for art class.

It took me a long, long time to fall asleep.

All week long I kept hoping that someone would magically find my notebook. I mean, it couldn't just have vanished into thin air! I kept my eyes peeled at school, even though it would've been terrible if a classmate had found the notebook. Worst of all, I remembered that I had written my name in bubbly letters on the first page. So if someone I knew found the notebook, they would immediately know that everything inside it was mine—including those Ewan sketches.

I made a mental note to self: *From now on don't write your name inside idea notebooks that are private. That way, if you lose it and someone finds it, you can pretend it's not yours.*

Actually, a second note to self: *Don't lose your notebook.*

On Saturday I had my cross-country meet in the morning. Then I procrastinated on my science project by patching up El Toro's busted seam. It didn't take long to finish, so I went downstairs to eat lunch. Finally I couldn't avoid it any longer, so I doubled down on my Felton Pier swings. I wanted to get them done and have Sunday morning to relax before work.

The swings were really frustrating me, but I was making progress when my phone chimed with a video chat alert. It was Sierra and Allie.

"Hey, girl!" said Allie as I picked up.

"What *up*, besties!" I said.

"Can you come over? We're making ice cream!" said Allie.

"At your house?"

"Uh-huh. My mom's at the shop, so we're doing this to surprise her tomorrow."

"Come, Miko! We need you!" said Sierra from behind Allie's shoulder.

Looking at the two of them together at Allie's mom's house, there was nothing I'd rather have done than join them. But I had mapped out my plans and wanted to stick to them. If I didn't work now, I'd pay later (and I had already procrastinated long enough).

There was also a teeny, tiny part of me that dreaded going over and hearing yet another conversation about Colin and crushes.

"This project is due Monday, so I really need to finish. Sorry, guys. Carry on without me. Call if you get stuck and need my help, okay?"

"Awww, okay. Love you!" said Allie.

"Love you guys!" I said. Then I hung up and turned back to the swing project.

I sighed loudly again. How was I ever going to finish it?

My dad appeared in the doorway. "Wow, Tamiko. That sigh was so loud that it shook the whole house."

Usually I had a witty response for everything, but today I just looked down at my hands. My dad must've noticed I was upset. He came into my room and sat down. "What's bothering you?"

"Everything sucks right now!" I cried. "There's this stupid science project that's taking forever, so I can't hang out with Sierra and Allie. And my idea notebook's gone, so literally anyone in the neighborhood could be reading all the stuff that's inside! And then there's all this talk about who likes who and who crushes on who, and everyone wants my advice on it. I don't understand why everyone has to be in love with someone else. Can't people just be friends? Why does it all have to be so complicated?"

"It seems like you have a lot on your plate." Then

my dad thought for a moment. "Well, there are many different kinds of love."

"What do you mean?"

"Well," said my dad, "some love is pretty straightforward, like the love you have for a pet. It's easy and uncomplicated. I have friends that I love too, but my family comes first. I love you and your brother and our family more than anything else. No ifs, ands, or buts about that. I am totally in love with your mom—crazy, silly, romantic love—and it's fun. But we can't always be silly. She's part of my family too, so I feel that kind of love for her."

I thought about my dad's words for a moment. It was true. I loved my family, but it felt somewhat different from the love I felt for my friends, like Allie and Sierra. It wasn't like one love was stronger or more important than the other. They were just different.

"Feelings can be messy too," my dad continued. "Sometimes you love someone and they might not love you back. Or maybe they love you, but not in the same way that you love them. People can also fall in love, and then out of love."

"Like Allie's parents?" I asked.

"Well, yes. Each relationship is different. For the Shears . . . they still care for each other and love each other as friends, but not as husband and wife. Sometimes love changes like that. But the love I have for you and your brother and your mom doesn't. It won't ever change, no matter what."

"Even when we make you crazy?"

"Even then. I love you more than anything, but when you don't clean your room, it makes me really crazy." He nodded his head at the pile of laundry on my floor.

I laughed. "Crazy love."

My dad laughed too. "Crazy love indeed!"

"Hmmm." I thought about Keiko being a little crazy because Ken hadn't gotten back to her. Then I thought about Emilia feeling kind of crazy because she wasn't sure if Carlo liked her. And Allie, wondering how Colin really felt about her. There seemed to be a lot of craziness and confusion and misunderstanding in love. And breakups, too. I thought of Allie's parents. That was sad.

"I've decided not to fall in love," I announced. "It's just too complicated."

"I think that's very wise for now. You can always

change your mind," my dad replied. "But in the meantime that doesn't mean you can't support people who are in love."

I considered that for a moment. "I guess. I guess it's not always a bad thing that people are in crazy love. It's just confusing."

"You're absolutely right about that!" My dad smiled. "But now let's see what we can do with this science project."

I made my dad promise that he wouldn't take over, then showed him the half-completed swings. He helped me hold the base while I attached the top, and he even had a few ideas to make it wobble less. Within a few hours the swings were almost complete! I felt a little silly for not asking for help earlier.

"Thanks, Tosh—I mean, Dad," I said. "Thanks for everything."

He gave me a quick squeeze, and it felt warm, like love.

Right before I got into bed that night, I realized that I had never responded to Keiko. I read her texts again and felt a little guilty for ignoring them. I didn't love Ken in the same way that Keiko did, but I still loved them both as friends and wanted them to be happy.

I texted her back: Sorry for the late response. I don't have a love life so idk what to say!!

Keiko responded right away: Don't be sorry. I just wanted to know what you'd do!

Hmmmm. I guess Allie and Sierra were right. Keiko wasn't coming to me because she thought I was a love counselor. She just wanted to know my opinion.

So I gave it to her, straight and unfiltered: Maybe you should just ask? There's no way to know unless you ask!

Keiko didn't respond for a few minutes, and I suddenly got a little nervous. Had I said the wrong thing? But then my phone buzzed with a new text: Thanks . . . you're totally right. You're the best. ☺

That made me feel good. I turned off the light and crawled into bed. Everything didn't suck, after all. My science project had turned out great, and I was even starting to feel better about this whole crush thing. I still didn't want a sweetheart, and I wasn't sure if I would ever want one. But I could still be there for the people who did. I imagined myself as a noble warrior, hands on my hips, standing up for all the people who were crazy in crushes. I liked that image. Maybe that would be the theme for my next art project: Tamiko Sato, the noble warrior for all kinds of crazy love!

## CHAPTER ELEVEN

# MORE THAN MEETS THE EYE

At the end of our shift on Sunday, Allie emerged from the freezer holding two Tupperware tubs.

"What are those?" I asked.

"The ice cream we made at my house yesterday," Allie replied. "We tried making some of the flavors on our list so that we could give my mom a taste test."

What an awesome idea! Mrs. S. came out from the back office. Allie and Sierra presented their two flavors.

"What are they?" asked Allie's mom, her eyes shining with excitement.

Allie filled four spoons and handed them around. "This one is Frozen Lemonade."

I examined the lump of yellow on my spoon. It

looked more like Play-Doh than ice cream.

Mrs. S. put the bite into her mouth, rolled it around, and then winced. "Wow! Sour!" She fanned her hand in front of her mouth.

I tried a small taste of my sample. Yes. Very sour. There was no way I was putting the rest of the bite into my mouth.

"Girls!" Mrs. S. laughed. "Did you put any sugar in this?"

Allie and Sierra looked at each other. "Yeah?"

"How much?" asked Allie's mom.

"Um? I don't know. A few teaspoons?" Allie said.

"Did you taste it?" Mrs. S. was grimacing.

Allie and Sierra laughed. "No! But it looked good," Allie said.

"What's the next flavor, dare I ask?" said Mrs. S.

Allie and Sierra laughed again. "Fried Pickle!" Sierra giggled.

Mrs. S. clutched her throat. "Ugh! I assume you didn't taste that one either?"

"Well, it looks good too," protested Allie.

"It's green," added Sierra.

"I'll try it," I said bravely.

Allie thrust another spoon at me, and I scooped

out a bite. The ice cream *was* green, and it was studded with pickle parts. This one also looked more like Play-Doh than ice cream.

"Here goes nothing!" I said, and I shoved it into my mouth.

It was pretty bad, but I really hammed it up. I pretended to gag, then rushed to the sink, then to the garbage, then back to the sink, as if I couldn't decide where to be sick.

"Tamiko!" squealed Allie.

"Just kidding," I said, wincing and swallowing. "But it is disgusting. How did you make it?"

"We fried a pickle. Then we put it into the blender and mixed it into vanilla ice cream. Then we added some mint ice cream to make it green," Allie said.

"Oh, and we mixed in pistachio ice cream too, because it didn't look green enough," added Sierra. "So there's some pistachio in there also."

"Wow. That is so gross!" I said.

"But it looks so good!" protested Allie.

"Looks can be deceiving!" said Allie's mom. "Just because something *looks* a certain way doesn't tell you anything about what's inside."

Mrs. S.'s words reminded me of what Mr. Rivera

had said about looking versus seeing. Just like Rocky Road—it might not look great, but it still tasted amazing.

Allie's mom cleared her throat. "The first rule of experimenting in the kitchen is to taste, taste, taste. It doesn't matter how pretty a food looks if it doesn't taste good. Also, you have to start with a basic ice cream recipe. And then keep track of everything you add in and how much. If you write down the combinations as you go along, then you'll be able to re-create the recipe."

"I don't think we'll want to re-create this flavor," I said.

We all laughed, and Mrs. S. said we should probably leave the flavor experimenting to her. We filled in Mrs. S. on all the other flavors we'd tried—what was popular, which stands had the longest lines, what little kids were begging their parents for. I still felt a little frustrated that I didn't have my notebook with me—there was probably some market research that we were forgetting. But we could tell that Mrs. S. was impressed.

"Nice work, girls! So, if you had to pick two flavors for me to experiment with—and by 'experiment,'

I mean do lots of *taste*-testing—what would you recommend?" She winked at us.

We all looked at one another, and then Allie said, "Hot Chocolate Marshmallow and Caramel Apple. *Amiright?*"

The three of us high-fived.

"I noticed today that with this cooler weather a lot of people have been asking for the hot caramel sauce," I said. "So maybe we do the Caramel Apple flavor as a sundae, with the chopped apples on top and a boatload of hot caramel sauce."

"Don't forget the sprinkle of happy," said Sierra.

"Never!" I said in mock horror.

Mrs. S. thanked us again. "I really think that introducing a new flavor will be refreshing and exciting for our customers. Maybe we can even create a sign in our shop window to draw people inside. And, Tamiko, once the new flavor is ready, can you please help me spread the news online?"

"Of course, Mrs. S.!" I said proudly. Mrs. S. wasn't tech-savvy, so I was the unofficial social media director for Molly's. That meant that I got to take a lot of beautiful photos and post them online to attract customers.

Just then the bell on the shop door jingled, and in walked Emilia and Carlo. Our shift was technically over, but the three of us rushed to the counter to take their order. Emilia ordered Peppermint ice cream, and Carlo ordered Rocky Road. They both seemed surprised and embarrassed to see us. They could barely squeak out what they wanted, they were so nervous. It was like they were worried that if they opened their mouths, they'd scare off the other person.

"Here's your sprinkle of happy!" I said, giving both of them more sprinkles than I usually did. It was the least that Tamiko, the lionhearted, crush-supporting warrior, could do to support their (what appeared to be a) date.

Emilia and Carlo sat down at a table and barely spoke to each other while they ate their ice cream. It was obvious that they found each other cute. There was lots of peeking and blushing going on—but barely any talking.

My first instinct was to roll my eyes, but then I looked more closely. Emilia *looked* silly. Her face was as red as the crushed peppermint in her ice cream. But I could also *see* that she was trying really hard to make conversation. And they were both smiling and seemed to be having a good time.

Then Emilia looked up from her ice cream, and we locked eyes. She had caught me red-handed, staring at them! But instead of looking horrified, Emilia smiled at me.

Hmmm. I guess sometimes impressions could be deceiving. I wondered if there was anything else that I was looking at but not seeing.

## CHAPTER TWELVE
# HAPPILY EVER AFTER

I took some extra time with my hair on Monday morning, arranging it just how I'd had it two weeks before, when we'd had our second art class for portraits. I put my granny dress back on, with the tights, the boots, and the biker jacket, and I made sure I'd packed my sketch pad for school.

My mom was driving me because I had to bring my science project and Sierra had some club meeting before first period. So I sat in the front seat of the van with the swings on my lap and sang along with the radio.

"I'm happy to see you in such a good mood on a Monday morning!" said my mom.

"Thank you, Ayumi. It is going to be a good day, I think."

"Okay, don't call me Ayumi. Why is that?"

"Well, my science project turned out pretty great. *And* Mrs. S. said she might have us come to the shop after school to try one of the new flavors we proposed, assuming she gets it done today. So I'll get to try some delicious ice cream and be all together with my besties—on a Monday!"

"Wonderful!" said my mom.

At school I dropped my project off in the science lab first, since there was no way I could fit it in my locker.

Mr. Franklin said, "Wow, Tamiko!" when I brought it in. Almost every other kid had done some kind of circuit board.

"I'm looking forward to your presentation in class today," he said.

"Me too, Mr. Franklin! See you later!"

I was in such a good mood that I almost didn't mind going to art class. Ewan was late to class. I kept looking at the door as everyone settled in, and even after Mr. Rivera said his little introductory spiel, Ewan still wasn't there! Mr. Rivera came over to my table.

"Tamiko, if Ewan doesn't show up today, you'll need to make a plan to meet with him outside of school so you two can work on your drawings."

*As if!* I wanted to say.

Luckily, Ewan came rushing in just then, red in the face, and grabbed a stool and pulled it over to where I was sitting. He mumbled "Sorry" to me and Mr. Rivera. Then he yanked out his sketch pad.

"Okay. I guess you're drawing first today?" I said.

"What? Oh. Yeah. Sorry. Um. Did you want to go first?" He could barely meet my eye. What was the deal?

I sighed. "No. You just go first."

He nodded and continued to draw. After a few minutes he seemed to settle down. "Did you get your bull home okay?" he asked, not meeting my eye.

Bull? Oh right. I had forgotten that he had seen me with El Toro. "Yeah. He's pretty giant."

Ewan flicked his eyes at me, then looked away. "Pretty sweet that you won him."

I nodded. Ewan put his pencil down and started rummaging through his backpack. Then he pulled something out.

It was my idea notebook!

"I can't believe it!" I nearly snatched it from his hands. "Where did you find it?"

Ewan blushed, and he looked down at his feet. "I found it on the bench right after I saw you with the bull last Saturday. I wanted to call you or text you, but I didn't have your number, and I was too embarrassed to ask your friends at the ice cream shop for it. I figured I'd just give it to you at school anyway."

"So why didn't you give it to me right away?" I asked, perplexed.

Ewan stared at the ground. "My parents are divorced. I stay at my dad's place some weeks, and then the other weeks I'm at my mom's. I forgot your notebook at my dad's house, and then I was at my mom's house until yesterday. I know it sounds really weird and complicated. . . ."

I shook my head. "No. My best friend's parents are divorced. I know how it is. It's not your fault."

He sighed in relief. "Thanks. I thought you'd want to kill me for taking so long to give it back."

"No. Thank you for finding it," I said. "I just wish you'd told me it was safe. I hoped it hadn't fallen into the wrong hands." But then I remembered . . . the *last* person I'd wanted to see this notebook was Ewan. Now my face was flooding with color. "Uh, did you . . . did you look at what was inside?"

"Well . . ." Ewan laughed in embarrassment. "Kind of. But I didn't read anything. I just . . . I kind of flipped through it."

I started talking a mile a minute. "The sketches of you . . . I just . . . They were the art assignment, but I didn't want to do them in the school sketch pad because I thought if you saw them . . . well . . . you'd think . . . and now you saw them anyway. Oh gosh. I feel like such a creepy person. I only did them for the assignment—"

"It's not creepy. I knew it was for art class," Ewan said. "Anyway, I'm glad your notebook is back with you now." Then he picked up his sketch pad and went back to work.

Sitting there silently, I examined Ewan. He still looked like the annoying popular kid who had thrown sprinkles at Molly's. But I felt like I had jumped to conclusions before actually *seeing* him. He wasn't a bratty guy who thought he was hot stuff. He was actually understanding and had been kind enough to return my notebook . . . even if I hadn't exactly been the nicest person to him.

"Okay. All done!" said Ewan. He folded shut his sketch pad and assumed his pose for me.

"Wait! I mean, you're totally finished?"

Ewan nodded. "Yup. I worked on it at home a little, so I was just tidying up some loose ends today. I'm done."

"Can I . . . Will you let me see it?"

Ewan's eyes twinkled mischievously. "Nope. You can see it on the wall at the art show."

"Ewan! Come on! I deserve to see it! I posed for it!"

"Fine." Ewan opened the sketch pad and turned it toward me.

I gasped. The portrait of me was incredible—it was so accurate that it was nearly a photograph. My head was tilted a tiny bit, giving me a sassy attitude, but there was a trace of a smile on my mouth. Then there was a sort of hazy glow all around me, and a pink to my cheeks and a brightness in my eyes that made me look alive in the picture. It had taken amazing skill, and I felt bad again for having assumed that he was a popular kid who thought it was cool to be bad at art.

But most of all I looked really, really pretty. Like, prettier than I'd ever thought of myself, even on my best day.

"Um . . . *wow!*" I said. Then I felt a slow grin taking over my face. "I love it."

Ewan smiled, and we high-fived. Being Ewan's partner had turned out to be a good thing after all.

Allie was already at the ice cream shop when Sierra and I arrived after school. They were both shocked when I told them who had found my idea notebook. But they were even more shocked to hear about Ewan's portrait of me.

"EWAN?" Sierra screamed. "Ewww, Ewan? He's a jerk!"

"Well, maybe he's not such a jerk, because he returned my book," I said.

"Wait, do you like Ewan?" Allie asked, her eyes widening.

"I don't like him!" I shot back. "Well, not in a romantic way."

"There's always more than meets the eye!" said Allie, trying to sound old and wise. I pretended to throw some sprinkles at her.

"Tsk-tsk, throwing sprinkles! You're starting to act like your boyfriend!" joked Sierra.

"He's not my boyfriend!"

"He was the only nice one that day, remember? He stayed to clean up, and then he left that money on the counter," said Sierra.

I was grateful that she'd remembered. It did make me feel better about Ewan that he'd done that. I didn't think I could be friends at all with the other two guys from that day. They were really jerks. But then again, maybe I had only been looking and not seeing them, too.

Allie looked thoughtful. "Maybe you should buy him a sundae the next time he comes in. Like, as a reward for returning your notebook."

"No! No free sundaes. He can buy his own sundaes."

"That's not a very nice way to treat your boyfriend!" said Sierra.

"Once and for all, he's *not* my *boyfriend*!"

We were all silent for a moment. "So no sundae for him?" said Allie in her meek little voice again.

This time we all had to laugh, even me. "No!"

We sat down at one of the tables in front, and Mrs. S. brought out a test batch of Caramel Apple ice cream. She served us like we were real customers, bringing us each our own bowl of the new flavor.

"Ready, set, go!" said Allie, and we all dug in at the same time.

"Mmmmm!" I said through a mouthful of ice cream. Then I chewed and swallowed. "Oh, Mrs. S., this is insane! It's tart like a real green apple, with a little bit of a crunch here and there—"

"That's the caramel coating the apples that I put in!" said Mrs. S. happily.

The caramel was amazing. It was like she'd folded actual sheets of caramel and then cut them into strips and mixed them in. They were more like solid caramel than just caramel sauce.

"This is incredible. I could eat this all day!" agreed Sierra.

"We just might have to, if it doesn't sell," Allie said.

"Let me SuperSnap this right now!" I said, whipping out my phone. My fingers flew over the keyboard.

"Girls! Let me take a photo of you all," said Mrs. S. "Hand me your cameras, please."

We handed over our phones, and she snapped a bunch of shots for each of us, smiling, with our spoons in the air.

"Besties forever!"

"Friends come first!"

"Even when we're old and gray!"

When Mrs. S. handed back my phone, I looked at the photo of us and smiled. I loved my Sprinkle Sundays sisters and would do anything for them.

I posted the shot of the three of us on my SuperSnap story. And I knew exactly what the caption would say: #CrazyFriendLove!

## DON'T MISS BOOK 6:
## *TOO MANY TOPPINGS!*

I checked the time on my phone as I hurried down the sidewalk—1:12 p.m. Whoops! I was late for my most important, most favorite activity of the week. Well, *one* of my most favorite activities. I had a lot of favorites. That was sort of the problem.

"I'm late! I know! I'm sorry!" I declared as I burst through the front door of Molly's Ice Cream parlor. The bell tied to the top of the door tinkled merrily, but that was the only merry thing that greeted me. My two best friends, Allie Shear and Tamiko Sato, were both in a whir of activity, taking orders and scooping ice cream.

Tamiko glanced up and gave me an icy stare, colder even than the ice cream. Ouch.

Even the customers in line seemed annoyed. Maybe I shouldn't have announced my lateness quite so . . . loudly.

I quickly tied back my long, curly brown hair and wished I'd thought of that on the way there. Customers didn't want hair in their food, and they probably didn't want to see me tying it back as I was dashing to the counter!

As quick as a flash, I washed my hands, donned an apron and a huge smile, and took my place at the register. I was the best at math, so I usually took the money and made change, while Tamiko, master marketeer, took orders and tried to convince customers to choose exciting new options that she often invented on the spot. Allie, whose mother owned the store, made the cones and shakes. We all did a little bit of everything, truth be told, but the three of us had been working together every Sunday afternoon for a few months now, and we'd gotten into a very comfortable and efficient rhythm of who did what.

There was no chance to explain my lateness with customers waiting. But with all three of us pitching in, we made quick work of the line and soon had the shop to ourselves. I took the opportunity to wipe down the counters, paying extra attention to the area around the toppings bar.

I felt really bad about being late. I wanted to apologize, but I was scared to bring it up, because I knew Tamiko and Allie would be mad. And I *hated* when my friends were mad at me. I was pretty sure I hated that feeling more than any other feeling in the world.

"Today must be your lucky day," Tamiko said finally.

I could hear the edge in her voice. It made my stomach queasy.

"What's lucky about being late?" I asked. I knew it was better to just say it than to try to pretend it hadn't happened.

"You're lucky because we were low on rainbow sprinkles, and my mom ran out to the store to get more before you got here," Allie explained. Her voice was less edgy, but I could tell she was annoyed too. "So she won't know you were late. Because we won't tell her."

"Yeah," said Tamiko. "You'll get away with it. Again."

The bad feeling in my stomach grew worse. I

didn't like getting away with something. I wasn't *trying* to get away with anything. I really wasn't.

"Thanks for understanding, you guys," I said. "I really do have a good excuse! My soccer game yesterday got canceled because of the rain and rescheduled for this morning. And then the game was 3–3, so we went into overtime . . . "

Allie sighed and rubbed a gritty spot on the counter with her thumbnail. "That's the problem, Sierra. You *always* have a good excuse."

"Since when is having a good excuse a bad thing?" I asked. I half smiled, trying to bring a little cheerfulness to the situation. After all, we were only talking about twelve minutes. Twelve minutes! I was sometimes much later for things.

Allie glanced at Tamiko. They seemed to have an entire conversation with their eyes in mere seconds.

Then Allie said, "Because I'm waiting for the day when you tell somebody *else* that the reason you need to leave early is because you have a responsibility to be at your job at Molly's. Which my mom pays you for. Why is everything else more important to you than being here?"

"It isn't more important!" I protested. "Really. I

love my job here—you know that. I'm just, well . . . I guess I'm just so used to being late that this isn't really that late to me. Anyway, I figured you guys would understand."

"We do understand—you're taking advantage of your friends," Tamiko said. "And it's not cool, Sierra."

Wow. Another ouch. This day was just getting worse and worse. Tamiko was always outspoken and said exactly what was on her mind, which I loved about her. But occasionally, when it was directed at me (or at one of my faults), it could hurt a little. But I couldn't deny that it was true: I did count on our friendship to keep me from getting into too much trouble. Working at Molly's on Sundays was my job. I needed to take it just as seriously as soccer and softball and student council and all the other things I did. Because they were all commitments I had made. And even more important, they were all so much *fun*. That's why I committed to so many things in the first place. I loved activities and meeting new people and being involved in lots of stuff. It made my head spin, but in a really good and exciting way. I was not the type of person to sit around. I liked to *go, go, go!*

Sometimes it was hard to explain that to people who liked things calm and structured, like Allie. Or precise and efficient, like Tamiko.

"Listen, you guys. I am really, really, *really*, truly, with cherries and Oreos and sprinkles on top, sorry. Okay? I'll stay later today to make up the time."

Allie sighed. "I know, Sierra. It's just that you've said that before."

Just then Allie's mom, Mrs. Shear, breezed in. "I'm back, girls!" she called, her arms full of economy-size tubs of toppings. "And they had so many yummy-looking things at the store that I had to try a few new things."

She went straight for the toppings bar and showed us the spiced nuts, lemon curd, nut brittle, and peppermint she'd bought. "Tamiko," she said, "I'll leave you in charge of coming up with interesting new treats that use these. You always have good ideas."

She patted Tamiko on the shoulder and flashed me a smile as she headed toward the back of the shop, where the storage and little office area were. We all called it "backstage."

"Now, I'll be backstage for a while doing some

paperwork, but feel free to come back if you need to talk to me," Mrs. Shear said. "And, Allie, please put some music on. . . . It's dead in here!"

Allie obediently turned on the store's speaker system and cued up a song on her phone. It was a fast-paced song and sounded out of place as my two friends and I stared at one another, not sure how to go on after our disagreement, especially since Allie's mom was back and might overhear us.

I was grateful they hadn't told on me, and truly sorry for being late. But I believed I had a valid excuse. I played right fullback on my soccer team, and my sub hadn't been there. I'd *had* to play. But there were *two* other employees here at Molly's working, and both were able to do the cash register. Was there something else they were mad about? Or was it really just my occasional lateness?

The three of us worked for a while in stony silence. Allie and Tamiko were stiff and awkward, and I felt so miserable that I debated whether I should just go tell Mrs. Shear I'd been twelve minutes late so that she could reprimand me. Maybe then my friends would let me off the hook. But if Allie had wanted her mother to know, she would have told her, and she hadn't. So I didn't want to get *her* in trouble for covering for me.

*Ugh.* It was all so awkward.

Finally an older lady came in and began studying the menu.

"What can I get you?" asked Tamiko, turning on her special Molly's charm. "We have lots of one-of-a-kind treats that aren't on the menu, so just tell me what you're in the mood for, and I'll make it happen!"

The woman, who was wearing a beautiful print scarf and pearls, looked amused. "One of a kind?"

Allie jumped in. "Yes! Here at Molly's all our ice cream is homemade, and we constantly have new items on the menu that you can't find anywhere else. Molly's is completely unique."

"I like unique." The woman smiled, studying us. "Are you three friends, or just coworkers?"

"Friends," I said quickly. "Best friends. They're my two best friends in the whole world."

The woman nodded knowingly. "I have two best friends too. We've known each other since we were kids. Three can be a hard number for friendships sometimes, but I'm glad to see you girls have it all worked out."

I didn't say anything, and neither did Allie or Tamiko. I wasn't sure we had it *all* worked out, especially today.

"I have a good feeling about you girls," the woman said. "How about you surprise me with something of your choice?"

Tamiko clapped her hands with joy, and with a sly look at me, whispered something into Allie's ear. Allie nodded and quickly got to work.

Tamiko told me what to charge, and I rang it up on the cash register. When Allie presented the woman with the finished product, a frothy milkshake made with three scoops of vanilla ice cream, flavored with spiced nuts, lemon curd, and peppermint.

"Mmm. It looks heavenly," the woman said. "What's it called?"

Tamiko beamed. "It's called a forgiveness float. Because even though friendships can sometimes be spicy or sour, forgiveness is sweet."

The woman took a sip and beamed. "Well done, girls. This tastes exactly like forgiveness—especially the little bit of lemon curd!"

She slipped a five-dollar bill into our tip jar and gave me a wink as she walked out the door.

"Thanks, you guys," I said, relieved to have been forgiven. "I mean it."

"You're welcome," said Allie. "Just don't make the forgiveness float a permanent item on the menu, okay?"

"Yeah," Tamiko agreed. "Promise us you won't add one more thing to your schedule, Sierra. You can't handle it, and we can't either."

I nodded vigorously. "I won't! I pinky-swear promise."

The three of us linked pinkies, and just like that, the day got better.

The next night, I was sitting at the dinner table with my parents, waiting for my sister. My family had a rule about not eating until everyone was present, so we were just waiting and waiting, with all my dad's delicious homemade Cuban cooking sitting in front of us, getting cold.

"Isabel!" Mom called. "¡*Ahora!* Now!"

I heard heavy footsteps on the stairs, and then a minute later Isa appeared in the doorway of the dining room. She was dressed in black from head to toe: black tights, black skirt, and a washed-out black T-shirt. Her expression was black too, like thunderclouds. I guess she'd been doing something pretty interesting up in her room. Not that I'd know what it was, since these days Isa and I hardly knew what the other one was doing.

It was pretty weird, especially considering the fact that we're identical twins.

"Who died, Isa?" I asked, trying to lighten the mood. I knew my parents were annoyed that she'd kept us waiting, and I was pretty sure her all-black ensemble would irk them too.

"Who died?" Isa repeated, giving *my* outfit—a bright yellow sweater, a jean skirt, and yellow socks—a withering look. "Your fashion sense. Obviously."

"Girls!" said Mom. "Not at dinner." She glanced at Dad and sighed. "Do you remember when they were little, and I had to fight to get them to wear different outfits because they always wanted to dress exactly the same?" She shook her head in disbelief.

Dad laughed. "I do remember. They were the two cutest things I'd ever seen. And I've delivered baby bunny rabbits."

Mom and Dad were both vets and ran a veterinary hospital together, so they always had great animal stories.

"The days of Sierra and me looking alike are long gone," said Isa, more cheerfully now. "Thank goodness." Then she looked pointedly at me. "Hey, Sunshine, can you pass me the salad?"

My face broke into a grin. Even when Isa really annoyed me, and lately it was often, I had to appreciate her sense of humor. Calling me "sunshine" because of my bright yellow sweater was pretty funny.

"Are either of you girls available to help at the hospital tomorrow after school? We're going to be a little short-staffed and might need an extra pair of hands."

"My science teacher is offering a special study session after school tomorrow to help kids prepare for our test next week," said Isa. "I need to go."

"And I've got my first rehearsal for the school play," I said. "Sorry. Maybe I can help you guys another day?"

Mom frowned. "I'm still not sure how I feel about you doing the play, Sierra. You've already got too much going on. Not to mention your regular schoolwork, which you need to keep up with. School has to come first, and with the play it all seems like a bit too much."

I forced myself to keep my voice calm. My parents didn't like it when anyone got hysterical at dinner.

"I understand, Mom, but I'm the lighting director for the play. I've already agreed to do it. And anyway, the show is in just a few weeks, and then it'll be over, so that'll be one less thing on my plate. Okay?"

Dad glanced down at my plate, which was still mostly full. "Right now I wish you'd eat a little something off *that* plate," he joked. "I worked hard on that ropa vieja!"

Dad's ropa vieja, which was Cuban-style shredded beef, was usually one of my favorites. But for some reason I just wasn't hungry this evening. I'd gotten home late from school because of softball, and I knew I had a long night of homework ahead of me. I felt all jumpy inside, and nervous, the way I did when I knew I had a lot to do and hadn't figured out yet how to do it all.

"Sorry, Dad," I said. "I guess I'm just a little distracted."

"Maybe the glare of your sweater is making you queasy," Isa suggested.

I rolled my eyes at her and made myself take a huge bite of the ropa vieja, then said, "MMMMMM-mmmm," really loudly to make Dad feel better.

"If you're too distracted to eat," said Dad, "then

you definitely need to rethink your schedule, Sierra. I don't think there's ever been a day in my life when I've been too distracted to eat!"

"Me neither," said Mom, squinting her eyes at me now and looking worried. "I really think you should—"

"Don't worry, Mami! I have everything under control. I promise. How about I go right up after dinner to do homework and organize my week, okay? I'll show you my planner, and then I can prove to you that I can get it all done."

"*Sí, sí.* That's a good idea. But I'm going to be keeping an eye on you. If I see you starting to look too stressed, we're going to have another talk. Deal?"

"Deal!" I agreed quickly, even though I couldn't believe how much everyone in my family was worrying. I was perfectly fine! This was just how I did things. It might not work for other people, but it worked for me.

After dinner I plopped down onto my bed with my backpack and school planner. I started filling in all the things I had to do that week, from lighting rehearsals, to sports practices, to Molly's, to homework. I hummed as I worked, which Isa always made fun of me for, but I couldn't help it. When I was concentrating or daydreaming, I hummed. During tests, during soccer games, even when I was watching TV sometimes! I sang in the shower too. I guess I had to always be doing *something*, and music was another thing that I loved.

After about fifteen minutes of moving things around in my planner, I made it all fit. I even slotted in time to study for that science test Isa had mentioned. We were in different sections but had the same test. She might even let me use her notes from the next day's special study session if I offered to do a few chores for her.

I really could get everything done! I wanted to rush downstairs and show my mother. But then my eyes fell onto a paper I had tucked into the folder pocket of my planner. It was the student council meeting schedule, and there was one the next day after school. There was no way I could make it, and I was the student council secretary. I had to be there to take notes.

Hurriedly I grabbed my phone and began texting everyone on the council, trying to find an alternate time to meet. I knew it was a big inconvenience, but hopefully everyone would understand. The play would be over soon, so this wouldn't affect the next council meeting.

After a lot of back-and-forth, and a few very snippy texts from the treasurer, we arranged to meet the next morning before school instead of after. I'd have to get up really early, which meant I couldn't study as much as I'd like for the science test tonight, but I'd still get to do everything.

I wanted to text Allie and Tamiko and tell them what I'd just done, and how I'd worked everything out without letting anyone down or making anyone late, but I didn't. I had more work to do first.

I focused on my homework and double-checked my planner twice to make sure I had included everything I needed to get to this week. I was ready to turn over a new leaf. I was going to still do all the things that I loved *and* get to them on time—because I really couldn't bear the idea of dropping even a single activity.

Playing softball and soccer made me happy because I loved both games (not to mention my teammates), and student council was a great way have a say in how our school was run, and last year's play had been so much fun! Everyone had joked around backstage and played pranks. And opening nights were spectacular. I didn't want to miss it this year. And Molly's—well, that was not just a way to earn a little money but also quality time with my two best friends.

Everything I did was part of who I am—yellow-sweater-wearing, humming, sunshiny Sierra. And I wasn't going to give any of it up. And I didn't have to! I just couldn't add any more, like Tamiko had said.

As I was climbing into bed I texted Allie and Tamiko. Good night, girls! I just scheduled my whole week in advance. I'm learning! You'll see!

Allie texted back right away: Yay! Glad to hear it.

Tamiko didn't respond. As I was closing my eyes I told myself she was probably just studying, or working hard on some art project. She was always bedazzling or redesigning something. Maybe I should ask her to help me redo my room.

*No, Sierra!* said a little voice in my head. *No more projects for now!*

# Still Hungry?

## There's always room for a Cupcake!

CUPCAKE DIARIES
Katie and the cupcake cure
1
by coco simon

CUPCAKE DIARIES
Mia in the mix
2
by coco simon

CUPCAKE DIARIES
Emma on thin icing
3
by coco simon

CUPCAKE DIARIES
Alexis and the perfect recipe
4
by coco simon

CUPCAKE DIARIES
Katie, batter up!
5
by coco simon

CUPCAKE DIARIES
Mia's baker's dozen
6
by coco simon

# sew zoey

Zoey's clothing design blog puts her on the A-list in the fashion world . . . but when it comes to school, will she be teased, or will she be a trendsetter?